The
Arrogant Guns

The
Arrogant Guns

LEWIS B. PATTEN

Thorndike Press • **Chivers Press**
Thorndike, Maine USA   Bath, England

This Large Print edition is published by Thorndike Press, USA and by Chivers Press, England.

Published in the U.S. by arrangement with Golden West Literary Agency.

Published in the U.K. by arrangement with Golden West Literary Agency.

U.S. Hardcover 0-7862-2192-5 (Thorndike Western Series)
U.K. Hardcover 0-7540-3975-7 (Chivers Large Print)
U.K. Softcover 0-7540-3976-5 (Camden Large Print)

The text of this Large Print edition is unabridged.
Other aspects of the book may vary from the original edition.

Set in 16 pt. Plantin by Al Chase.

Printed in the United States on permanent paper.

British Library Cataloguing-in-Publication Data available

Library of Congress Cataloging-in-Publication Data
Patten, Lewis B.
    The arrogant guns / Lewis B. Patten.
        p.   cm.
    ISBN 0-7862-2192-5 (lg. print : hc : alk. paper)
    1. Large type books.   I. Title.
    [PS3566.A79A89 1999]
    813'.54—dc21   99-41715

The
Arrogant Guns

CHAPTER 1

At daybreak, the first of the low black, swift-scudding clouds had appeared, sailing like ships of war down the sky out of the northeast. They came singly and in small groups at first, but before an hour had passed, before the sun had a chance to poke its rim above the horizon, they filled the sky on all sides as far as the eye could see.

Thunder rolled ponderously, and an occasional bolt of lightning slashed earthward, to sear a scrubby pine on a high point of land or to shatter a rock and leave it crumbled, smoking, and hot in the suddenly humid air.

The rain came, accompanied by howling surface winds that ripped at the split-cedar shakes on the roof of the tiny railroad station, that sent everything that was loose rolling across the station platform.

Matt Wyatt stared broodingly through the streaming window. The train wouldn't be arriving for a couple of hours yet. If Matt Wyatt had his way it would never come. Because its coming would set off more violence than this part of New Mexico had witnessed yet. It would start a war, small perhaps as most wars went, but big enough for Matt. Big enough for Colonel Lafferty too.

A war of insurrection, thought Matt sourly. A war that would, in the end, cut Colonel Lafferty down to size and destroy what was left of him just as the lightning destroyed everything it struck.

He turned his head and stared at the colonel sitting on one of the benches over against the wall. Lafferty was staring at the floor between his feet, looking in this moment like a small Napoleon.

Size, thought Matt, maybe Lafferty's size was behind it all. He was sensitive about it, certainly. And perhaps his need to prove that his size wasn't everything had driven him like a goad all these many years. Perhaps the goad had made him accumulate the things he had, land, cattle, enterprises that ranged from packing houses and tanneries to textile mills and his own private wild West show.

Impatiently Matt fished in his pocket for tobacco and papers. He rolled himself a smoke with strong, brown fingers that trembled slightly, licked the paper, and stuck it into his mouth. He wiped a match alight on the seat of his faded jeans and touched it to the end. Hell, the colonel even had his own spur railroad line, branching off the main line and running the length of monstrous Two-Bar ranch to serve his packing plant and tannery, his sawmills up in the timbered country to the north, and his marble quarry in the rocky peaks beyond. This station was on that spur line and was called Two-Bar Station.

He turned and crossed the musty room. He glanced briefly at the Mexican woman waiting with her five children for the train, then passed and sat down at the colonel's side. "How many did Saxon say he hired?"

He knew the answer to the question and wondered why he had asked. He supposed he was still trying — to talk the colonel out of this foolhardiness, to stop this ruin before it was too late.

"Forty-seven. Counting Les and you and me it makes fifty men."

Forty-seven. Forty-seven, chosen for their ability with their guns, chosen because, for a price, they would do exactly what the man paying it told them to. Some of their names Matt knew. Some, he had never heard of before. But they would come, and pile off the train, and mount the saddled horses waiting in the rain out in the loading pens. And they'd follow Colonel

Lafferty and Matt across the boundary which, the colonel said, separated Two-Bar and the territory of New Mexico. They'd start Lafferty's war of insurrection.

Matt's mouth twisted wryly. The history books would probably call it Lafferty's War. And they would record its defeat, the slaughter of Lafferty's fifty men including Matt and the colonel and Les Saxon.

But they wouldn't record Matt's memories. They wouldn't record the things that had driven Colonel Lafferty to this point. They wouldn't record the twenty-five years that Matt had been close to the colonel, the years that compelled his loyalty even in the face of certain disaster now.

Perhaps the colonel was a little mad. He would have to be, thought Matt, to do something as obviously ruinous as this. Mad with power. Mad with bitter disappointment in his son. Mad, because in spite of all he had built out of nothing here, he had failed in his personal life.

Or at least he thought he had failed. Matt felt differently. He stared at the brooding face, seeing its fiery strength, its implacable determination even in repose. Colonel Lafferty *was* a Napoleon. Only instead of having a nation to work his will upon he had only the empty reaches of New Mexico.

A small chill touched Matt's spine. Nervously he got up and paced to the window. Rain was coming down in sheets, beating against the flimsy station, pouring from its eaves, forming lakes in the flat land beyond the tracks. Matt suddenly wanted to kick something. He wanted to pound somebody with his fists.

It went back a long, long way. It went back to a burned adobe house somewhere south of here on the vast, brushy plain of Texas. And Matt's face suddenly twisted with that memory.

Nearly twenty years ago, it had been. And one of his earliest memories . . . Yet he remembered something violent and terrible that had happened even before Colonel Lafferty came. . . .

He remembered a river, not a cool, blue river but a hot, brown one running sluggishly through a land overgrown with brush. He remembered a house built of adobe that was cool even on the hottest days. . . .

And a woman, who must have been his mother. A worn, tired woman dressed in homespun. And a man that always reeked of sweat and whose skin was like creased and wrinkled leather from the time he spent working in the sun.

He remembered . . . Only vaguely did he remember the night of the Comanche attack. He had felt his mother's fear and that of his father. And he had been terribly afraid himself.

An hour before dawn they sent him out of the house alone, with admonitions to make no sound, to creep along the ground until he reached the thick, thorny tangle of brush behind the house.

He recalled crying because he did not want to go. But in the end he went, and crept along the ground silently as if he were playing a game. He reached the tangle of brush and lost himself in it, lying as still as a newborn fawn all through the terrible things that happened afterward.

There were shots, and shrill cries, and once a sound from a horse so shrill and awful it was like a woman's scream. Later, there were human screams — those of his mother — and moans — and finally silence that was, in its way, more terrible than the sounds had been.

All that day, Matt lay almost motionless in the tangle of brush. And all the following night, although he was thirsty, and cold, and hungry too.

The wind changed during the night, blowing from the house toward Matt, and he smelled the biting smoke that came from its smoldering embers. At dawn he stumbled out of the brush tangle, not crying now, but pale and terrified and shocked by the things he saw . . . the bodies of his mother and father . . . the blackened ruins of the house . . . the wantonly slaughtered chickens and pigs . . . the emptiness of the corral where his father's horses had been . . .

He was five. He was old enough to find two partially burned blankets and cover his father's and mother's bodies with them. He was old enough to poke through the still-smoldering ruins of the house until he found some food, and old enough to pull up a bucket of water from the well.

But he wasn't old enough to decide what he should do or where he should go. So he stayed, scavenging food from the cooling ruins of the house, drinking water, growing used to the smell of death that became worse with every passing day.

Even now he could not have said how long he was there after the attack. But at last one day he was awakened and looked up to see a man, a small-statured man dressed much as his father had dressed and riding an enormous black stallion whose hide gleamed and shone in the early morning sun.

Matt got up, knuckling the sleep from his eyes. He wanted to cry with relief but he did not. Instead, he said, "Injuns kilt my ma an' pa. I hid."

The man stared at him for a long, long time, scowling as though he was angry. Then he got down, tied his horse, found a shovel with half a handle and began to dig two graves.

He worked in silence for most of the morning, while Matt sat on the ground and stared solemnly at him. Then he wrapped the two bodies in the rags of blankets and rolled them into the graves. Only when he had filled them in did he turn and look at Matt. "Guess I'm stuck with you, kid. Come on."

He lifted Matt to his saddle and mounted behind him. He rode away toward the north.

The days passed, mostly unremembered except for the food that was plentiful now. The land fell away behind the huge stallion and the undersized pair riding him. Once or twice the man said to Matt, "I don't know what the hell I'm goin' to do with a little kid. Guess I'll try and find some Mex woman that'll take you in. Ain't no white women this far north, that's for sure."

Matt would feel cold whenever the man

talked to him this way. And scared. But he never did anything but clench his jaws.

Up out of Texas they came, riding by night as they passed through Comanche country and reaching at last the Spanish and Pueblo settlements of New Mexico.

One evening at dusk they stopped at a small adobe trading post, where the man bought ammunition and supplies with gold from a small leather bag. There were three other men at the post, bearded, hard-eyed men who frightened Matt. Afterward they rode out again.

They camped a dozen miles west of the trading post and the man picketed his horse to graze. They ate and wrapped themselves in blankets and lay down beside the fire to sleep.

Matt awoke to the stealthy noises first. He stared wide-eyed into the darkness at the lurking shadows moving so quietly toward his protector's horse. He yelled. . . .

There was a flurry of movement out there. . . . Beside him the man threw off his blankets, was up like a cat and charging away into the night. . . .

Shots — and shouts — and cries of pain. . . . To Matt it was like the night of the Comanche attack. Only different too because when it was over the man came back, reloading his long-barreled pistol and grinning at Matt in a way he never had before.

"Guess maybe I'll keep you after all. If you hadn't yelled . . . well hell, we'd a been afoot, that's all."

He stared at Matt for a long, long time. At last he knelt and put out his small, strong hand. "I'm Dan Lafferty. What's your name, kid?"

"Matt."

"Matt what?"

"Wyatt, I guess. That's what my ma always called my pa."

"That musta been his first name, Matt. Don't you know what his last name was?"

Matt shook his head. Lafferty said, "Matt Wyatt it is, then. Let's get up and get out of here. I killed one of those men out there. The others might come back."

Lightning flashed brilliantly in the tiny railroad station. The windows seemed to glow with it. Matt strode to one of them and stared through its streaming pane. A tree across the tracks a quarter mile away was smoking, afire from the bolt. There was a streak down its trunk where the bark had been ripped away.

Thunder cracked, rattling the windows, seeming to shake the floor upon which Matt

16

stood. Two of the Mexican woman's small children began to cry.

Matt turned his head and stared at Colonel Lafferty. The man's head had not raised. He seemed oblivious of the storm.

Suddenly, remembering the way he had been those first few years, Matt could see how much he had changed. His hair, that of it which showed beneath the wide brim of the shapeless cavalry style hat he wore, was graying now. Matt knew it was thin on top.

The face was heavier, holding none of the lean strength of youth it once had shown. The eyes were deep-sunken, and troubled.

But the jaw — that never changed. Strong and hard and jutting almost challengingly. Matt remembered that it had always been that way.

How he had acquired the beginnings of Two-Bar, Matt didn't know. Perhaps he had bought it with the small amount of gold he had. But Matt knew how he had come by the first cattle he stocked it with. He'd spent several months with three hired Mexican vaqueros catching wild horses in the badlands two hundred miles west of here. He'd driven the horses south and when he returned after trading with the Comanches on the Staked Plains he had a hundred and fifty head of wild-looking Texas cattle. He left

Matt with the wife of one of the vaqueros while he was gone.

The cattle ranged free, for there were no other ranches or settlements for fifty miles. They ranged free, and bred, and increased as the years went by.

And Matt grew. He grew stringy and strong as rawhide. He rode like an Indian boy, bareback, balancing himself precariously but expertly because his legs were too short to grip the horse's barrel the way they should.

He rode with Dan Lafferty. And because there was no one else to talk to, Lafferty often talked to Matt.

Sometimes he seemed almost to be talking to himself. Many of the things he said, Matt didn't understand. He was too young. But he liked the sound of Lafferty's voice. Unlike his body, Lafferty's voice had never been small. It was deep and booming, as though it ought to be coming from a man twice his size.

Matt learned early that Lafferty's driving ambition was as much a part of him as his size. "This land is mine, Matt," he would say, waving his short arm in a wide circle. "As far as your eye can see and even farther than that. Wherever Two-Bar cattle walk, the land is mine. I took it an' I'll keep it. It ain't worth enough now to tempt anyone to try takin' it away from me. By the time it is . . . well, by then we'll be big enough to give 'em all the scrap they want."

Matt listened, and rode, and worked as hard as any man. He continued to grow and as he did, something grew within him that was almost like worship of Lafferty.

But there were drives in Lafferty that Matt would never understand. Not until he was older and had experienced them himself. The time inevitably came when Lafferty could no longer live alone. He needed a woman and he left the ranch to look for one.

This time there was no one to look after Matt while he was gone. So he stayed alone and looked after himself. He learned not to fear the silences or the black of night. He decided that there were only men to fear and discovered that the cold smooth feel of a gun beneath his hands drove away that fear.

IIc was eight that year. He was eight and while Lafferty was gone he took an enormous old Dragoon Colt Lafferty had, loaded it, and went out into the yard to practice shooting it.

The first time he fired it, he thought it had broken his arm. He sat down on the ground, staring at the smoking gun, feeling tears beginning to form behind his eyes.

But they never materialized. His damp eyes hardened. His small jaw firmed and clenched. He got up and raised the gun and held it with both hands while he fired it again — and again — and again.

Lafferty was gone two weeks. By the time he returned, Matt could hit a rock a hundred feet away from him with reasonable regularity, though he still had to hold the gun in both his hands.

Staring out through the station's streaming window, a small grin formed on Matt's wide mouth. For an instant the worry left his eyes and they filled with memory.

The woman Lafferty brought home — Matt had thought her wonderful at the time, with her strong fragrance, her black net stockings, her silken gowns. He hadn't known Lafferty took her out of a saloon in Albuquerque. He hadn't known Lafferty married her less than an hour after meeting her. Nor had he known that Lafferty had chosen her the way he would choose a mare — for the length of her legs, the breadth of her shoulders, the width of her hips and the ampleness of her breasts. He'd chosen her to bear a son and to ease the hungers that tormented him in the night.

Matt turned his head and stared at the colonel's face. If he'd chosen her for other things — and more carefully — he might not now be here awaiting the destruction he felt compelled to start. If he'd chosen someone else his son might have . . .

Matt shrugged fatalistically and turned to stare along the railroad tracks. What was done was done. No amount of hindsight could change things now.

CHAPTER 2

Matt didn't suppose he would ever forget the day Lafferty brought his new wife home. He grinned with the memory, seeing her climbing down from the buggy in his mind, seeing the look of utter consternation on her face.

The house in which Lafferty and Matt had been living was a hastily constructed, two-room shack built of adobe bricks fabricated right here. Matt and Lafferty had built it themselves, assisted by a couple of Pueblo Indians, hired when they stopped for water and paid for their trouble with a bony, dry cow.

The roof was of stout timbers covered with brush and after that with sod. At the time of Lafferty's arrival with his bride, it had been raining several days. The sod was almost thoroughly soaked.

Lily stood in the pouring rain, staring at the sea of mud and at the squat, ugly adobe house. Over behind it was the frame shack that had been here when Matt and Lafferty came. It was used for storage now.

White-faced, Lily whirled and confronted

Lafferty. "You son-of-a-bitch! I thought you was rich! You let me think it too, you son-of-a-bitch!" Tears formed in her eyes and her mouth trembled.

Lafferty, standing half a head shorter than she, turned and waved an arm. "I told you I had land. I have got land. All the land as far as you can see. I said I had cattle and I have. Thousands of 'em. I didn't say I had a damn parlor house out here."

"Well you will have, you lyin' little runt. You will have or I won't stay!"

Matt remembered the way Lafferty's face had frozen tight as she said the word "runt." He remembered the ice in Lafferty's voice. "Then start walkin' back to Albuquerque. Because I ain't going to drive you back."

Lily sat down on the muddy stoop in the front of the door. Her silken skirt lay unnoticed in the mud. She began to cry.

Lafferty stared at her furiously for a long time. Matt was scared. He wanted to run but he didn't know where to run. He felt sorry for Lily and thought she was pretty in spite of the way the rain had made her hair droop on both sides of her rouged face. She didn't exactly remind him of his mother, yet she made him think of her. He looked at Lafferty hopefully.

Lafferty drew a line in the mud with the

toe of his boot. "Aw hell, let's don't fight. Come on inside and stir us up something to eat. You'll have a better house. Give me time and you'll have every damn thing you want."

She looked up, her face streaked with tears and rain, smudged on one cheek with mud. She stood up haughtily, her eyes taking on a certain resignation. "Well, I just better have. And I ain't going to wait forever, either."

Lafferty crossed to her. Short as he was and tall as she was, he lifted her easily. She giggled and squealed, "You just keep your hands where they belong."

Lafferty carried her inside. Matt followed, lighted the lamp, and began to build a fire in the stove. He kept glancing from one to the other uneasily.

The meal was plain but it was hot. As soon as it was dark Lafferty and Lily went to bed in the other room.

Late in the night Matt awoke to the sound of steadily dripping water leaking through the thick sod roof. Shortly thereafter, he heard Lily cry out, and then begin to scream at Lafferty to wake up.

Lafferty awoke and grunted something heavily in his deep voice. Lily screeched about the leaky roof. Lafferty got up and lighted the lamp. He said softly and disgustedly, "Tonight! By God, tonight! It ain't never leaked before and it's got to start tonight!"

Lily continued to rail at him. He stood it for almost half an hour. Finally he dressed himself and stamped outside. Matt heard the reckless pound of his horse's hoofs as he rode furiously away. He heard Lily crying bitterly in her soggy bed. . . .

A bad beginning for a marriage. It began with quarreling and it continued that way until its end. Lily and Lafferty quarreled in the morning, at noon when he and Matt came in for dinner, and at night. Or at least most nights. There must have been some nights they didn't quarrel for Lily began to grow heavier and when she did, her tongue became more sharp. She would scream at Lafferty often nowadays. "You damned little runt, if you don't build me a decent house, I'm going back to the saloon in Albuquerque and have your brat!"

At last Lafferty gave in and began construction of the house. It was neither easy nor quick. Lafferty had no money and in order to get some, he had to round up a herd of steers and drive them to Santa Fe. He and Matt returned with a veritable wagon train of supplies, and with a gang of Indian laborers.

25

Construction of the adobe bricks started first, consuming mountains of clay and endless wagonloads of tough prairie grass. Great piles of cured bricks grew. Lafferty laid out the house and the walls began to rise.

Materials continued to arrive from Santa Fe and Albuquerque and from the high mountain country where spruce grew straight and tall. Sometimes Lafferty would disappear for a week, returning with a great collection of notes and drawings of buildings he had seen and from which he wanted to copy certain things.

The well was in the exact center of a huge courtyard that was, itself, paved with adobe bricks. The house was built U-shaped around the courtyard, which was closed at the open end by an adobe wall.

On the three sides of the house that faced the courtyard, a wide gallery ran, its roof supported by long spruce poles extended inward to support the roof of the house and its second story.

The main floor of the house was paved with stone, as was the floor of the gallery. The walls, at their base, were three feet thick.

It was completed finally, six months after it had begun. And now furniture began to arrive, heavy, handmade furniture Lafferty had bought in Santa Fe.

The floors were covered with Navajo Indian rugs, and many of the walls were hung with them. Lily was in her ninth month of pregnancy. In spite of that, invitations went out to everyone within two hundred miles. And at last the great day came.

Matt could not remember seeing so much food at one time, before or since. A steer and several pigs and lambs were kept turning on spits over a bed of coals by Indian laborers. The ovens in the enormous kitchen of the house had been going full blast for days. Great long tables had been set up in the courtyard, in the shade of several trees Lafferty had hauled from the mountains in wagons and replanted there. Mexican and Indian women moved back and forth endlessly between courtyard and kitchen.

Lily tried to oversee it all, her face shiny with sweat and sometimes twisted with either pain or fatigue.

It was a cool, crisp day with a bright sun and no clouds. Lafferty dressed in his best and paced the long gallery waiting for the first arrivals.

The sun climbed across the sky. Lafferty's pacing continued. Noon came, and went, and a flush appeared in Lafferty's face. His eyes were like stone, his mouth a thin and angry line.

Lily came out onto the gallery and quarreled with him in a shrill voice that carried from one end of the courtyard to the other. Matt went out a dozen times an hour to scan the empty horizon, looking for their arriving guests.

But no guests came. The afternoon waned, and the sun sank toward the western horizon. At last, near nightfall, Lafferty ordered the Indians and Mexicans to dig in and eat their fill.

Matt could stand it no longer; he could not bear the look on Lafferty's face. He got himself a horse and rode out, away from the monstrous house, away from the reveling, half-drunken Indians gorging themselves in the huge courtyard.

He rode for miles, for hours it seemed. And at last he rode back, obsessed with a feeling of uneasiness, of dread. For what Lafferty might do. For what Lily might do.

He heard her screaming while he was still a quarter mile away. He heard her screams over the continuing sounds of revelry in the firelit courtyard. He fell over the sprawled-out body of a drunken Indian as he came through the huge, oak gates.

The screams came from an upstairs window of the house. They would stop for a while, and then begin again. During the silences between, Matt would hear Lafferty's deep voice, though he could not make out what Lafferty said.

The sounds of revelry died in the courtyard. Those of the merrymakers who could still walk staggered out, to their own squat adobe houses a quarter mile away. And at last, Matt heard the lusty wailing of a baby.

It was not really surprising to Matt, now, that Lafferty's son turned out the way he did. His mother had carried him in hate. She had taught him hate from the time he was able to understand.

They named him Lincoln, which was promptly shortened to Link.

He was a lusty, strong baby, who, when he cried, could be heard from one end of the huge house to the other. But Lafferty saw little of him. He became increasingly grim as the days and weeks and months dragged by. He was never at home unless he had to be. He drove himself endlessly, and drove Matt, and drove the dozen or so Indians and Mexican cowhands who worked for him nowadays.

When he was at home, Lily and he quarreled. Matt would hear her screaming taunts at him, taunts about his size, taunts about other things Matt did not understand. Matt sometimes wondered how long it would be before Lafferty murdered her.

He turned his head now and stared at the colonel, sitting with his head sunken on his chest at the far side of the railroad station. He left the window and crossed to him. He sat down.

He wanted to say something. His own memories had made him feel a kind of nostalgic sadness and perhaps he understood that the colonel was feeling the same way. He said, "I've been thinking. About . . ."

Colonel Lafferty glanced up. His eyes met Matt's and passed on. Matt finished, ". . . about Lily. She was good at hating and she taught Link how."

Lafferty smiled faintly. "She didn't hate me, Matt. I couldn't see it then, but I can now. She was just scared . . . that she'd always be what she was when I married her. She thought everyone knew and she believed they'd never forget. She was defiant enough about it to prove to them that they were right."

His head dropped onto his chest. His eyes stared blankly at the Mexican woman waiting for the train. But the faint smile remained on his lips.

Matt got up, feeling helpless and ineffectual. Lafferty had loved Lily, incredible as it seemed. Even now he felt compelled to try to understand her and to make excuses for her.

But Lafferty was wrong about Lily. She *had* hated him. And she had taught their son to hate. His father. The people who had failed to accept Lily's invitation. Everyone who had ever hurt her in any way. Lily was dead but her hate lived on in Link.

And soon Link would be dead as well. The colonel's attack on the forces of civilization was doomed to failure.

The storm still beat ferociously at the flimsy station as though trying to blow it away. Matt stared out the window absently.

Those early years had not been pleasant ones for Matt, and though time had softened things for him, it still hurt to remember. Lily was angry and Lafferty was both baffled and hurt. He stood it for about six months before he moved out of the bedroom he shared with Lily and their son and into a small room opening off the gallery and all the way to its end.

But the colonel was right about one thing, thought Matt. Lily had seemed determined to prove to the country's inhabitants that their estimate of her was right. After he stopped living with her . . .

He frowned, remembering the one time Lily had softened and confided in him.

"They're right, Matt. I'm just what they think I am. My folks got taken by the smallpox when I was thirteen. A real nice old gentleman and his wife took me in to help her with the housework because she was sick. The first thing the nice old gentleman did was get me in bed with him. And that's where I stayed until I got old enough to get me a job in a saloon."

She was silent for a time, saying at last, "Don't be like them, Matt. Don't be like the rest of the sons-of-bitches are. Treat a woman like she was a human being, not like some kind of trash to be used and thrown away."

Matt said stoutly, "Lafferty ain't like that."

"The hell he ain't!" But her face relaxed almost immediately and she said so softly that he could scarcely hear, "No, he ain't like that. I know he ain't. Only it's too late for me to change. I try to treat him nice and the first thing I know I'm screechin' at him like a fishwife. He hates me now and I guess I can't blame him much."

Matt was silent, puzzled, and confused. Being good to someone seemed like such a simple thing to him. You either wanted to or you didn't. He couldn't understand someone wanting to and not being able to.

He left her uneasily. Lily had puzzled him then and she puzzled him now. But he knew it was possible for a person to blame someone else for his own feelings of wrong-doing and failure. It was possible for Lily to hate Lafferty because she couldn't stand to go on forever hating herself.

As soon as young Link was weaned, she began driving to San Juan, a small Spanish settlement thirty miles away. She would stay for several days sometimes, coming back disheveled and sick.

But in spite of Lily, in spite of Lafferty's obvious misery over the state of things, the work at Two-Bar went on. There was never an end to it. Matt realized now that Lafferty had buried himself in it to keep himself from doing something violent.

Yet even the work had not prevented the violence when it came.

CHAPTER 3

Visitors rarely came to Two-Bar. When one did it was enough to make everyone notice. The Indians, the Mexicans, and Matt, if he was around the house, would stare and speculate upon the visitor's business here.

Jack Lane was no exception. He came riding toward the ranch house from the direction of San Juan one afternoon, whistling and glancing around interestedly. He waved cheerily to Matt as he passed through the gate, and flashed an engaging smile.

He was tall, and sat his horse straight and easy like a cavalryman. He wore a black hat with a flat brim that was like a Spaniard's hat and yet was not. The crown of this one was high, rounded and uncreased. His suit was also black, like a suit Matt had seen on an undertaker once when he was in San Juan with Lafferty.

He wore a gun that seemed incongruous on one so carefully dressed otherwise. It was a huge old Navy .36-caliber Colt, carried in a sagging, weathered holster around his waist. All of it except the polished grips showed beneath the lower hem of his coat.

His shirt was white, and had ruffles in the front. He wore a narrow black tie and his feet were encased in polished black boots on the heels of which were great Spanish cart-wheel spurs.

He dismounted at the main door of the house and handed the reins to an Indian boy. He raised the huge knocker and let it fall.

Lily answered the door. She seemed startled at first, then flustered, but she finally invited him in. The heavy door closed behind him.

He did not reappear until long after it turned dark. At the door he turned, spoke to Lily, and flashed his smile at her. He waited, leaning indolently against one of the gallery posts until his horse was brought to him. Then he mounted easily and rode unhurriedly away.

Matt saw Lafferty watching from the shadows of the gallery at its end. He saw Lafferty go inside and close the door.

Matt was eleven that year and his head was filled with the dreams common in boys that age. He worshiped Lafferty, but he was fascinated by the dashing appearance Jack Lane presented to the world. Lane became what Matt wanted to be, and he began to ape the mannerisms of the man.

Lane returned frequently, but not until his fifth or sixth visit did he meet Lafferty. The meeting was strained. Lafferty was cold and civil. Lane was smiling and affable, yet beneath his affability a certain strain was visible. After the meeting, Lafferty began to wear a gun regularly, a fact which puzzled Matt.

At eleven a boy finds it difficult to understand the machinations of adults. He had not understood Lane's coldly calculated purpose, but apparently Lafferty had. Lane was courting Lily, right under Lafferty's nose. Not because he wanted Lily, although she apparently thought he did, but because he wanted Two-Bar ranch and was willing to gamble his life for it.

Anger was always noticeable in Lafferty whenever Lane was around. And once Matt asked, "You don't like him, do you?"

Lafferty shook his head.

"Why not? Because he's comin' to see Lily instead of you?"

"Ain't proper for a man to go callin' on the wife of another man. Not unless that man is dead."

"Why don't you tell him not to come?"

"Because it wouldn't do any good. He'd keep coming because he's got a plan."

"What do you mean, a plan?"

Lafferty's face was grim. "A killin' plan. He's shinin' up to Lily so's she'll marry him when I'm dead."

Something cold touched young Matt's heart. "But you ain't going to be dead!"

Lafferty smiled at him. "Maybe. Maybe not. I expect Jack Lane's pretty fast with that gun he packs."

"You think he'd shoot you?" Matt's voice was incredulous.

"I know he will. He's just waitin' for the right time. And he'd like me to start the fuss. It'd look better to Lily that way."

"What about . . . you could get the sheriff, couldn't you?"

"Not his fight. Besides, what has Jack Lane done? What's he done that's the sheriff's business?"

"Nothin', I guess." Matt couldn't believe it. He said, "You sure that's what he's fixin' to do? Shoot you, I mean?"

"I'm sure, Matt. And I'll give him his chance when the time for it comes."

"Couldn't you have him . . . ? Well, you got a lot of men around here working for you. They'd do anything you told 'em to."

"Yeah. I could have him killed. Or whipped. But I wouldn't think much of myself if I did. No, I guess I'll just have to play this Lane's way. Whenever he's ready,

I'll be ready too."

The deadly game went on, while Matt watched in horror. And at last, one night, Lane stayed through the night.

Matt awoke at dawn as he usually did, and came out onto the gallery in his bare feet, rubbing his eyes. He headed across the courtyard toward the pump.

He noticed Lane standing in front of the big main door, staring toward Lafferty's room at the gallery's end. He jerked his head around and saw Lafferty step out onto the gallery.

Lafferty was fully dressed. He even wore his hat. His gun was strapped around his middle, and the bottom of the holster was tied to his leg.

Matt's chest felt as though there were ice in it. Instinctively perhaps, or because of the way both men looked at each other, he understood that the time had finally come.

Not until many years later did he completely understand Lafferty's willingness to play Lane's deadly game. It was a matter of pride, and was tied in both with Lafferty's small stature and with his love for his faithless wife. Lafferty could have handled Lane in any of a dozen ways without danger to himself. Yet he understood that by so doing he would lose what little respect Lily might have left for him. And he would lose his self-respect.

Lafferty stepped off the gallery and the sun struck him in the face. He stepped quickly back, then began to pace evenly along the gallery toward Lane.

Lane was pale. His face was almost as white as a woman's face. His eyes were narrowed against the glare of the sun on the courtyard paving. His mouth was a thin, hard line.

He remained motionless, letting Lafferty come to him, taking this tiny bit of advantage shamelessly. A careful man. A man who gambled but who seized every available chance to win.

Matt glanced at Lafferty's face. It was stolid, without visible expression. It seemed completely normal except for the towering anger in his eyes. Lafferty said, "You son-of-a-bitch, you stayed the night with her!"

Lane nodded. "I did. What are you going to do about it?"

"Kill you. That's what I'm going to do."

Lane smiled lazily, but the smile was forced. "You can try, little man. You can try. Where do you want us to bury you?"

Matt glanced from Lane's face to Lafferty's. It was pale now with fury. His hand, hanging close to the grip of his gun, was twitching. Matt shouted, "Don't let him make you mad! That's what he's tryin' to do!"

Lafferty didn't look at Matt. And he didn't reply. But a certain steadiness seemed to come to him and Matt knew he had heard.

Lafferty reached the "L" in the gallery and turned. No obstructions now stood between the two. The distance was only about fifty feet.

Lafferty paced on steadily, a step and a pause, another step and another pause. Each time he paused, he steadied his weight on both feet.

Matt had never seen him so tense. Yet his movements were liquid, like those of a cat as it stalks a bird.

Matt glanced back at Lane's face. There seemed to be no color in it now. The eyes were narrowed. Lane licked his lips.

Lafferty laughed when he did.

It was a soft laugh but it was filled with triumph and with mockery. Lafferty had broken Lane's nerve. With his own stolidity, with his own careful, steady pacing, he had made the moment stretch out until the strain of waiting became too much for Lane.

Matt kept his eyes glued to Lane fascinatedly. He saw the conflicting desires

40

that crossed the man's face. Lane wanted to quit but he just plain didn't know how he could.

And Lafferty gave him no opening, no chance to back away gracefully. When only twenty-five feet separated the two he stopped. He didn't speak. He just waited, watching Lane's face coldly.

When Lane moved, his hand was like light. If Matt had blinked, he would have missed the whole thing. One instant Lane was standing there straight, the next he was crouched and his gun was in his hand, firing, roaring obscenely on the quiet sun-washed gallery.

But another gun was firing too and its sound was deeper, throatier. It was Lafferty's old .44.

Lane's body twitched as the first slug took him in the shoulder. He was driven back as the second slug took him in the chest. He twitched again and fell as the third cut a leg out from under him.

He fell onto the paved gallery, spilling his blood onto it and triggering his gun reflexively until it was empty.

Matt was afraid to look toward the place where Lafferty had been. He stood there staring at Lane's still body as though he were hypnotized. Lafferty's voice was soft, almost gentle when it came, "Matt. Look over here. It's all right, Matt."

Matt's tears came in a flood. His face contorted and he couldn't compose it however hard he tried. He began to shake, a shaking that began in his knees and traveled upward until his whole body was shaking violently.

He could hear a woman screaming and saw Lily come from the door and throw herself down beside Lane's bloody body. But she was blurred because of the flood of tears in his eyes.

And suddenly there were strong arms around him and his face was buried against Lafferty's powerful chest. It smelled of horse, of sweat, of tobacco.

Lafferty held him so tight Matt thought his ribs were going to break. But the trembling stopped. And so did the flood of tears. Lafferty's deep, booming voice said hoarsely, "I said it was all right, Matt, and it is. He didn't touch me."

He released Matt and turned back toward the gallery. Matt followed him like a dog, still not believing. Lane had seemed so fast. . . .

He got a glimpse of Lafferty's face as the man stopped beside his kneeling, weeping wife. Lafferty said harshly, "Get up!"

She looked up at him, her face wet with

tears. She struggled to her feet. She swung a hand at him, but he caught it with one of his own. She tried to claw him with the other, her face twisting with more fury than Matt had ever seen in her. Lafferty caught that hand too.

He held her there inflexibly for a long, long moment, staring impassively into her face. Then he said harshly, "Go in the house. And don't come out of it again. If you do, I'll kill you like I killed him."

Lily turned and went into the house without uttering another word. The door slammed violently.

A crowd had collected by now, a crowd composed of Two-Bar's Mexican and Indian cowhands and their families. Lafferty said, "Get him out of here. Bury him someplace. And clean up the goddam gallery."

He walked back along the gallery to his room at its end. He went inside. And he did not emerge again until afternoon.

Matt stared at the closed door for a long, long time. In him was a kind of awe. He wondered if he, himself, could ever face what seemed like certain death without showing a trace of fear.

Two of the men carried Lane's body past him, limp and bloody. A woman drew a bucket of water from the well and began to clean up the blood on the gallery floor.

Matt went out of the courtyard and got himself a horse. He mounted and rode aimlessly across the plain.

Lafferty had been so cold — so sure. . . . And yet when it was over he had been gentle as any woman could have been with Matt. . . .

Matt hoped that when he was grown he could be half the man Dan Lafferty was. What he didn't know was that in the next few years he was going to have to grow up mighty fast.

CHAPTER 4

This was New Mexico, hundreds of miles removed from the stirring conflict between North and South. Yet even here the rumblings were audible.

There was a newspaper in San Juan, its editor a man named Wilhite, originally from South Carolina. When that state seceded from the Union the newspaper carried enormous headlines announcing the fact, although the news did not reach San Juan until early in January.

The newspaper was a weekly, and each week, now, more than half of the news was concerned with the increasing tension between North and South. At last, in April, the paper announced, again in screaming headlines, that the South had taken Fort Sumter.

Matt had never seen a slave. He did not understand the causes lying behind the conflict, all of them at least. But apparently Lafferty did. He was gone from the ranch much of the time now, attending meetings in San Juan, Albuquerque, and Santa Fe. Though he had been raised in Texas, his sympathies were solidly with the Union, which, he felt, should not be split in two.

Matt later understood that another strong reason behind Lafferty's enlistment was his misery over Lily. But there was a third reason. Again Lafferty had to prove himself. He had to prove that his stature wasn't everything.

And so, one day, when a troop of cavalry on patrol from Fort Union stopped at the sprawling house at Two-Bar, Lafferty gathered together a few of his possessions, mounted his huge, gleaming sorrel horse, and rode away with them.

Before he went, however, he called Matt into his room at the end of the gallery.

Matt had begun to shoot up, and was already taller than Lafferty though he was only twelve. He was lean and stringy, but he was strong and he knew the vast miles of Two-Bar range as well as Lafferty did.

Lafferty stared at him speculatively for a long time before he spoke. Then he said, "You ain't much more'n a kid, but you're a damned good kid. I hadn't ought to leave but . . . Hell, Matt, I got to leave. I got to go. Can you see that?"

Matt nodded uncertainly.

"Reckon you can look after things?"

Matt nodded stoutly, though the thought

of it turned him cold.

Lafferty stared at him doubtfully. He shook his head. "No. I guess I can't go after all. You just ain't old enough."

Matt said, "I am too old enough. I can sell cattle if we need money. I can do what I been doing all along." He was thinking in terms of Lafferty being gone for weeks, maybe for months. But not for years.

Lafferty strode to the open door and stared at the Union troops milling in the bright courtyard. He glanced back at Matt.

Matt saw a strange expression in his face just then. A look of resignation. As though Lafferty had already relinquished Two-Bar ranch. As though it were already lost to him.

He said brusquely, "All right. If you say you can do it, you go ahead and try."

The troop was mounting in the courtyard at the shouted command of one of its officers. Lafferty gathered his things and ran. He turned and waved at Matt, and he glanced once at the main door of the house. Then he mounted and rode out of the courtyard gate without looking back.

Matt stood alone in the center of the courtyard and watched him go, enveloped by the cloud of dust the horses raised. He walked to the gate and stared after the departing troop until it disappeared.

Then he swung around and stared toward the main door of the house. Lily was standing in it, but Matt couldn't see what expression was on her face. She had not been out of the house for months. Now she came out, blinking in the bright sunlight, carrying her baby in her arms.

Matt crossed the gallery and entered Lafferty's room. He wandered around it, now and again touching some thing that had belonged to Lafferty.

Something close to panic was growing in his heart.

He picked up Lafferty's .44 lying on the bed and stared at it. He laid it down, took the cartridge belt and holster from a nail on the wall, and belted it around his waist. It was several inches too big so he punched new holes in it with his knife and tried it on again. He slid the gun into the holster and felt its solid weight pulling against his waist.

He felt as though Lafferty had deserted him. He felt more alone than he ever had before in his life. He felt his chin begin to tremble and his eyes begin to burn.

Then he remembered the day Lafferty had faced Lane out on the gallery. He remembered wondering if he would ever be the man Lafferty was. He clenched his jaws and blinked back the tears.

He might fail. Two-Bar might fall apart. But it wasn't going to happen because he hadn't tried. Or because he quit.

He went out, got himself a horse, and rode aimlessly the rest of the day, alone on the plain. He wouldn't have to do anything he hadn't been doing all along. The only thing missing would be Lafferty's strong hand on the reins.

His uncertainty lasted for about a month. After that he never thought of it again.

Lafferty was at Fort Union for a month. He wrote back once while he was there. The next letter Matt got from him was post-marked Chicago. After that there was only silence for months. The San Juan newspaper carried news of the Federal defeat at Bull Run in huge headlines. It also carried news that a local man, Dan Lafferty, had been promoted in the field to captain.

There were more months of silence. Then a letter from Lafferty, telling Matt a little of the battle, but saying nothing of his own part in it, or of his promotion. The letter was gloomy and after reading it, Matt was sure the Union would soon lose the war and Lafferty would come home.

But the war continued and Lafferty did not come home. General Sibley marched up the Rio Grande from Texas, was defeated at Glorieta Pass near Santa Fe, and retreated frantically back down the Rio Grande.

The banner headlines in the San Juan newspaper appeared less often now, for there were seldom Southern victories to report. Northern victories were reported in small articles on page two.

Matt passed his thirteenth birthday and his fourteenth.

He saw little of Lily these days. Her son played in the courtyard, watched by Maria Chavez, the wife of one of Two-Bar's cow-hands, and Lily spent more time in San Juan and Albuquerque than she did at home. She would come back sometimes looking as though she had slept in her clothes for a week, sick and red of eye. She would not reappear for several days. Then she would drive away in her black buggy, to be gone again from a few days to several weeks.

Lafferty was promoted to major. But at Two-Bar life went on unchanged.

The cattle herds increased as the years went by. Each spring, Matt rode for several months doing nothing but catch, brand, and castrate calves.

Even with the eight Indians and Mexicans who had remained at Two-Bar, the task was seldom finished before midsummer. When it was finished, another task began, that of moving herds from one section of Two-Bar range to another where the feed and water were better. There were mountains on the north rim of Two-Bar, and here the cattle spent the summer months.

When fall came, they were returned to the lower country. Usually in the fall, Matt and the others gathered several hundred steers and drove them either to Fort Union or to Albuquerque, where they were sold. And in the winter they stayed close to ranch headquarters, repairing saddles, mending harness, repairing buckboards and wagons, and breaking horses to ride.

Matt's eyes lost their youthful look. They were very steady and calm these days. At fifteen, he was almost six feet tall and looked as if he were in his twenties at least. Except for the light fuzz that had begun to appear on his bronzed and weathered cheeks.

He wore the old .44 Colt yet, and he wore it now the way Lafferty had worn it the day of the fight with Lane. Sagging on a cartridge belt. Tied around his leg just above the knee. He practiced with it a little every day. But he never forgot the lesson he had learned the day Lafferty fought with Lane. He worked harder at hitting his target than he did at getting the gun out fast.

In the fall of 1864, on a crisp October day, a man came pounding into the courtyard at Two-Bar riding a worn-out, barebacked horse. The man was nearly hysterical. Comanches had attacked the town of San Juan, he said, and had killed eight people before they were driven off. The man was one of a half a dozen riders sent to warn outlying ranches in the area.

Fortunately Lily was at home. Matt watched the rider leave on a fresh, Two-Bar horse, then crossed the courtyard to tell her.

She was alone in the huge living room. Link was beating on the floor with a hammer not far from where she sat.

It was the first time Matt had talked to her in many months. He stared at her a moment, seeing the lines the years had put around her eyes, seeing the changes her way of living had put into her face. There was an unhappy look about her mouth and broody dissatisfaction in her eyes. But they warmed as they looked at Matt and she smiled uncertainly.

Matt cleared his throat. "Comanches attacked San Juan last night. Killed eight people before they were driven off. You'd better stay in the house for a while."

There was no fear in her face. Her eyes

showed no touch of it. She said, "Sit down Matt. Sit down for a while. It gets so damned lonely here sometimes and you're always busy someplace or other."

He sat down uncomfortably on the edge of a chair. She asked, "What do you hear from Dan?"

"Nothing. I haven't had a letter for several months. Last I heard he'd been promoted to major."

"He never writes to me."

Matt stared briefly at her. He glimpsed hurt in her, and a kind of forlorn disappointment. He caught himself feeling sorry for her, but when he remembered Lane . . . when he remembered the times she had stumbled into the house looking as if she had spent a week lying in an alley someplace, his pity faded.

She asked, plainly trying only to break the awkward silence, "How are things going?"

"Fine. Fine. I guess there are twice as many cattle as there were when he left." He sat there uncomfortably for several more moments. Then he got up, turned uneasy by the way her steady glance rested on his face. He said, "I'd better close the gates and see that the men have ammunition enough."

He went out, feeling strange whenever he remembered the way Lily had looked at him. He shook his head angrily.

He gathered the men and their families and brought them inside the courtyard. He had all the horses driven into the courtyard, where they were rope-corralled.

Lily came out onto the gallery and watched the preparations from there. Light faded in the sky and the velvet night came down.

Lily disappeared, but a while later she came out again. She had changed her clothes, had put on a fresh-looking gingham dress and had fixed her hair. She called softly, "Matt."

He crossed the courtyard to her. She said, "Would you eat with me tonight, Matt? I get so tired of eating alone. And I've fixed something you'll like."

He started to refuse, then stopped. His own feelings when he was near her troubled him and made him want to get away. But he experienced a return of the pity he had felt toward her earlier. Right now she didn't look capable of conspiring with Lane to kill her husband. She didn't look capable of carousing around San Juan for several days at a time.

Fifteen. In any other environment Matt would still have been a boy. Here he was a man, doing man's work, as big and strong as any man. And he was reaching the stage in his development where women would become a necessity to him.

He washed and returned to the house. He went in and sat down at the table with Lily and with Link, who was noisy and bad-mannered. Lily at last put the boy to bed in exasperation.

She returned, and they finished eating, and afterward sat awkwardly groping for things about which they could talk.

She asked, "Do you think the Comanches will get this far?"

He shrugged. "I doubt it."

"If there were enough of them to attack San Juan . . ."

He said, "There's nothing to worry about." But there were faint memories stirring in his mind. Of a small adobe shack deep in the hot Texas plains. Of a man and woman who had been his father and mother. Of a screaming, violent attack and later the smell of death and the naked bodies of his parents lying in the sun.

He suddenly felt a little sick. He said, "I'd better go out and see if everything's all right."

She pouted. "You don't like me. You don't want to talk to me." But her eyes rested warmly on him and again he felt the strange uneasiness he had experienced before.

He went out, surprised to find that he was sweating heavily. He crossed the courtyard, opened the gate and stared into the darkness outside.

He wondered if he was afraid. He felt clammy and cold and something was lumping violently in his stomach. His hands shook slightly.

What would Lafferty do tonight, he wondered. What would Lafferty do that he hadn't already done? He went over his preparations in his mind and decided there wasn't much else he could do.

He told himself they probably wouldn't come here anyway. They probably wouldn't have come this far.

But there seemed to almost be a smell in the air of the night. The hairs on the back of his neck stirred uneasily. Behind him, one of the horses nickered shrilly.

Matt closed the gates and dropped the heavy bar into place. There were Indians out there even now. All they waited for was dawn.

CHAPTER 5

The hours of night dragged slowly past. Matt paced back and forth along the gallery. He stared at the wall across the open end of the courtyard. It wasn't high enough. It wouldn't even slow the Comanches down. They'd come over it howling and Matt's few men would be overwhelmed. Nor was the house impregnable enough to make a stand in there. It hadn't been built with Indian attacks in mind.

Matt wished he knew how many Comanches there were. He knew there might only be a few, a small group instead of the entire war party that had attacked San Juan. But it wasn't likely.

He tried to decide how Lafferty would meet the threat. Then he shook his head impatiently. Lafferty was away fighting in the war. What was done here tonight would be Matt's doing. Now, tonight, he had to forget Lafferty and stand on his own two feet.

The faint, unwelcome memories of the murder of his parents kept recurring in his mind. Numbers of this bunch of Coman-

57

ches might conceivably have participated in that attack, he thought.

His anger began to stir, but in spite of anger, some of the near-panic stayed in the back of his mind. He scowled.

Why were the Comanches now raiding so far north? There had to be a reason. One reason, of course, was that the manpower of the frontier had been depleted by enlistments in the armies of the North. The garrison at Fort Union was smaller than it had ever been.

But what did the Comanches want?

He suddenly felt almost weak with relief. The Comanche wanted what he had always wanted. Horses. That was the reason for this raid. Horses were as scarce on the frontier as were men.

The air was chill now. Chill was approaching dawn. Matt crossed to the courtyard gate, climbed up and peered over. He stared into the blackness intently, trying to see something, anything.

Gray slowly began to spread upward from the horizon in the east. There were shapes out there. . . .

He dropped back to the ground. He lifted the bar and called softly, "Drop that rope corral. Mount up."

The rope that corralled the horses

dropped. The bunch spread out over the whole courtyard. Matt walked to where his own saddled horse stood and swung to his back. The men grouped around him uneasily.

He said, loud enough for them to hear but not loudly enough to be heard outside the wall, "There's only one thing a Comanche wants. Horses. So we'll give 'em these. We'll wait until we hear 'em coming. Then one of the women can open the gates and we'll drive these horses out. Maybe they'll forget the attack and go after the horses instead. I don't figure even a Comanche will risk gettin' killed if there's no profit in it for him."

There were soft grunts of approval from the men. They knew they'd be overwhelmed, thought Matt. They were as willing as he to grasp this straw.

He returned to the gate. Two women stood by it, waiting to swing it wide. By standing in his stirrups, Matt could just see over its top.

He could see the Comanches plainly now. There must be fifty of them. They were grouped, but as he watched, they spread out into a single file. For a moment, they sat their horses, motionless.

Matt felt a sudden hatred so strong it

made him want to vomit. This same tribe had butchered his parents, had orphaned him. Damn them! Damn . . .

The line surged into motion. There were high yells from the oncoming braves. Weapons, rifles, lances were brandished in the air. Dust rose from the horses' hoofs.

A quarter mile . . . They halved that distance in a few short minutes. . . .

Matt roared, "Open the gates!" his changing voice coming out deeply and without breaking. The gates swung back. . . .

He yelled, "Drive 'em out!"

Inside the courtyard there was suddenly a volley of shots, a chorus of high, wild cries. The frightened horses broke toward the gate.

Crowding, biting, kicking, squealing, they streamed on through. Matt rode to the wall, stood high in his stirrups and peered over.

The charging line of Comanches had stopped uncertainly. The last of the horses went out and the gates slammed shut. The bar dropped solidly into place.

Matt bawled, "Man the wall!"

The men rode to the wall, crowding their horses close to it, raising in their stirrups to peer over it.

Manes and tails whipping in the wind of their own making, the loose horses thundered away, at right angles to the line of Indians facing them. The Indians' hesitation vanished. They thundered in pursuit. Matt watched until both horses and pursuing Indians had disappeared over a rise of ground.

He swung from the back of his horse, opened the gates, and stared into the pall of dust. He was soaked with sweat although the air was chill. He began to shiver violently.

But he knew that he had won. He had traded thirty or forty horses for the lives of all those here at Two-Bar.

Tension broke suddenly within the courtyard. Women began to cry, and laugh, and the men shouted uproariously. Lily stood in the doorway of the house, watching Matt.

He crossed to her. Her face was pale. Her lips were trembling. She had been more frightened than she had been willing to admit, he realized suddenly.

She said softly, "Matt, come in. You and I both need a drink after that."

He went in reluctantly. She got a bottle from a cupboard in the kitchen and brought it in, along with two glasses. She poured each of them half full.

Matt didn't want a drink. He'd never

tasted any but he'd smelled it and hadn't liked the smell. But neither did he want to refuse.

He took the glass, raised it to his mouth and drank it as though it were water. Instantly his throat felt as if it were on fire. He gagged, made a face, then gasped for breath. When he got it, he began to cough.

His eyes filled with tears, he glanced at her. She wasn't laughing at him. She had no smile on her lips. She was watching him in a way that suddenly scared him more than the Comanches had. Her glass was as empty as his. She said softly, "Wait a minute, Matt. Then have a little more. It won't make you choke this time."

He should have left immediately. But the way the whiskey had overcome him made him feel like a little boy and that angered him. He'd show her . . .

Warmth from the first drink was now spreading in his stomach. A strange feeling of relaxation and well-being began to seep through him. He watched her as she poured his glass half full a second time.

He drank that one more slowly, a mouthful at a time. He succeeded in keeping his face straight, neither choking nor gagging nor coughing this time.

His head felt light. He watched her

without protest as she poured his glass half full a third time. He drank that too, then said, "I've got to go out. . . . They might come back. . . ."

She said softly, "You were wonderful, Matt. You're not a boy any longer. You're a man."

He felt himself smiling foolishly and he couldn't seem to stop. She came over and sat next to him on the sofa. He could smell her strong perfume and edged away . . .

She whispered, "You're afraid of me, aren't you Matt?"

"Me? Why should I be afraid of you?" His voice was defiant.

"I don't know, but I think you are."

"I am not!" The warmth had spread all through him now. His whole body felt warm and strong, but his head felt light. It reeled and he saw two of each object in the room. He shook his head but it did not clear.

She was closer now. Her perfume filled his lungs and made his chest feel tight. And suddenly her arms were around his neck, her lips lightly brushing against his own.

He pulled away violently and got to his feet. He swayed dizzily. He knew suddenly that he had to get out of here. He had to get away. Yet something seemed to be trying to drive this bit of reasoning from his mind, something that threatened to overwhelm him, to which he must not give in.

Lily got up and came toward him. Matt hesitated, wanting to stay yet knowing he must not. Abruptly he turned and bolted from the room.

He plunged through the front door and onto the gallery. It was full dark now and the courtyard was deserted. From beyond its wall he could hear the faint strumming of a guitar.

He felt a strange compulsion to turn and go back inside in spite of the fact that he was afraid, in spite of his conviction that it would be wrong.

Whether he would have done so or not, he never knew. The decision was taken out of his hands. Lily came to the door and began to screech angry curses at him.

He ran along the gallery to his room. He went in, slammed and barred the door. He fell across the bed.

Guilt made him burn with shame. He told himself that he had done nothing wrong, yet he knew that if Lily had not begun to scream at him when she had, he might have gone back inside.

What would she tell Lafferty when he returned, he wondered fearfully. And what would Lafferty do when he had heard her lies? He suddenly remembered Jack Lane and the way Jack Lane had died.

Shivering occasionally, he lay awake all night, staring blankly at the dark ceiling of his room.

CHAPTER 6

The Comanches did not return. One of the Indian cowhands trailed them fifty miles south, just to make sure they did not intend a second attack. Afterward, life at Two-Bar went on much as it had before.

With one outstanding difference. Matt was very seldom at home place nowadays. He avoided it like a plague.

Not that Lily would have bothered him, but he did not know this. She had needed a man the night of the Comanche attack and Matt had suddenly attracted her. There had been no more to it than that.

Much of the time, he slept in the open underneath the stars. But as time passed, he began to see the need for cabins, or line shacks as they were later to be called. He had them built at intervals all along the edges of Two-Bar range. And he supervised Two-Bar from one or another of these shacks.

Lafferty was promoted to colonel, but Matt never received a letter from him any more but what he thought of Lily, tormented himself with guilt, and wondered what she would tell Lafferty when he returned.

As the cattle increased, so did the need for men increase. And as the number of Two-Bar employees increased, so did Matt's difficulty in properly supervising them all. He was forced, finally, to return to the house in order to do it efficiently.

Lily paid no more attention to him than she had before the night of the Comanche attack. Matt's guilt began slowly to fade.

Young Link was seven now. He was a moody, sullen boy who looked neither like Lafferty nor like Lily. He was tall for his age, had black, straight hair and dark eyes. His skin was sallow from spending too much time indoors and his face was thin, as though he did not eat enough.

Matt came and went from Lafferty's room at the end of the gallery. And a succession of men came and went from the house.

Matt paid little attention to them, for they were not his responsibility. Some, he knew, were fortune hunters aware that Lafferty might be killed before the war came to an end. Others — Lily even used her powers of persuasion on the cowhands, be they Mexican, Indian, or American. Matt always fired them when he found out, but it never stopped Lily.

At sixteen, Matt was capable of discharging anyone he didn't want around. They invariably took it sullenly, but not one ever offered Matt a fight. The gun that hung always at his side . . . they knew how accurate he was with it. Nor did they seem anxious to stand up against his hard-boned fists.

But there were two . . . Manuel Vargas and a Texan, Lucas Payne. Matt didn't know either of them had been seeing Lily. He couldn't have stopped what happened even if he had.

It was winter. Snow lay thinly across Two-Bar range, crusted from the previous day's thaw. Matt was in his room at the end of the gallery, working on the ranch accounts.

He heard a shout in the courtyard and raised his head. He got up and went to the door.

There were lights over in the house. There was a man standing before the big front door, a gun in his hand.

Matt didn't recognize him immediately. He turned, got his own gun and belt, and strapped it on. He went out and walked toward the man.

He recognized the man as he approached. It was Manuel Vargas, who had been hired about three months before.

Vargas was almost as tall as Matt, but more slightly built. He had a way of keeping an eye on the horizon when he was working and Matt had decided he was wanted, someplace, by the law.

Right now he was very drunk. He was shouting at Lily to open up the door. He was demanding that Lucas Payne come out.

Matt approached him from the side. He said thinly, "Put it away and come draw your pay. Be off Two-Bar by dawn."

Vargas whirled, bringing his gun to bear. When he recognized Matt, he let his arm fall to his side. He asked drunkenly, "Don't you care what's going on in there?"

Matt asked sourly, "What's going on in there?"

"Payne's in there with her. That's what."

"What the hell do you care? She ain't yours."

"She . . ."

Matt said wearily, "You were told to stay away from the house. I guess you didn't hear. So let me tell you something about her. She's through with you. She's got Payne now. But she won't have him to-morrow because he's leaving just the same as you." His voice turned sharp and cold. "Now put that damned thing away and come draw your pay."

Vargas stared at him sullenly for a moment. Then he reluctantly holstered his gun. He shuffled toward Matt's room.

Matt paid him the amount that was due. He stood in the door and watched Vargas shuffle through the courtyard gate.

About ten minutes later the house door opened and Payne came out. Matt waited until the door closed, then called, "Payne."

The man came across the courtyard toward him. Matt handed him his pay. He said, "Get on your horse. Be off Two-Bar by dawn."

He was angry. He felt disgusted and a little sick. But he was glad Lafferty wasn't here.

Payne took his pay silently, and shoved it into his pocket without counting it. He said, "Trespassin', huh? On your private . . ."

Matt hit him then. Squarely in the mouth. He felt teeth crack beneath his knuckles.

Payne staggered back, slammed against one of the gallery supports, and slid to the stone-paved gallery floor. He got up painfully, spitting blood and bits of teeth. He started to say something, then changed his mind. With a murderous look at Matt, he turned and staggered toward the courtyard gate.

Matt went inside and closed the door. He rubbed his bloody knuckles on his shirt.

He put away the account book and blew out his lamp. He stirred the fire in the stove and added another chunk of wood. Then he removed his clothes and got into bed.

He lay awake for a while wondering if the war would ever end, if Lafferty would ever come home. Then he fell asleep.

He slept hard. But when he wakened it was with a violent start.

He sat upright in bed, for an instant wondering what had wakened him. Then he was on his feet, charging for the door, snatching up his gun and belt as he went.

Clad in long underwear, barefooted, he ran across the courtyard on which half an inch of fresh snow lay. He saw tracks, boot tracks, heading toward Lily's door, but saw none coming away. He drew the gun from its holster and thumbed the hammer back.

He reached the door just as Vargas came backing out. He clipped the man solidly on the head with the barrel of his gun. Then he stepped inside.

He could hear young Link sobbing. But from Lily he heard no sound.

The great living room was dark. He crossed to the table, found a match and lighted the lamp. He lowered the chimney and looked around.

Lily lay sprawled half on the stairway, half on the floor at the foot of it. Link was standing halfway down, staring at her with horror-stricken eyes. She was clad in a nightgown. And there was blood. . . .

Matt picked up the lamp and crossed to her. She was breathing, but her breathing had a choking sound.

She stared at Matt and tried to speak. She choked and began to cough. The coughing stopped suddenly and her body went limp. Her head fell back. . . .

He glanced up at Link. He rose, stepped over Lily's body and started up the stairs.

Link turned and fled. Matt heard a door slam violently upstairs. He hesitated on the stairs a moment. There was nothing he could do for Link, nothing he could say. Lily was dead. Nothing would ever change that fact.

He wondered if Link had seen her killed. Not that it mattered much. Vargas was the guilty man. And Vargas was going to hang.

There were others in the room when he went back downstairs. Lily's cook, Elena. Maria Chavez, who had taken care of Link for several years. A couple of cowhands who had also apparently been awakened by the shot. Matt nodded his head toward Vargas, lying in the door. "Tie him up. We'll take him to San Juan tomorrow."

Lily's body had been covered with a blanket. Matt looked helplessly at Maria. "Will you dress her and get her ready, Maria? We'll take her to San Juan when we take Vargas in."

He didn't want Lily buried on Two-Bar range. He didn't want her grave anywhere near, where it would remind him, where it would remind Lafferty too if the colonel ever returned.

Maria nodded. Matt, suddenly conscious that he wasn't dressed, hurried to the door and crossed through the thin snow to his room. He dressed, and stared moodily, emptily at the wall for a long, long time. When Elena brought his breakfast, he drank the coffee but ate nothing. He was glad when the sky grew light.

He went out and had two wagons harnessed. He detailed two men to drive the wagon with Lily's blanket-wrapped body in the back. He himself drove the one with Vargas in it, trussed like a chicken ready for the oven. The man was conscious now, but he did not say anything. He knew what was to come and had apparently accepted it fatalistically.

The sheriff of San Juan County was a

dark-faced man named Jaramillo. He cut Vargas' bonds and herded him into a cell. He listened to Matt's story impassively, his expression saying that what had happened was inevitable.

There was no one at Lily's funeral but Matt and the men who had driven her body in. After the brief service, Matt accompanied the hearse to the San Juan cemetery and watched her casket lowered into a grave.

She was gone. With her was gone the possibility that she would lie to Lafferty about what had happened on the night of the Comanche attack.

His feelings about her, as he drove back toward Two-Bar, were conflicting and confused. He was glad she was dead, for she had been evil and would have continued to be. Jack Lane was dead because of her. Vargas would soon die because of her. She had driven Lafferty away, and Lafferty might yet be killed because of it.

And yet, young as he was, Matt understood as well how Lily had been tormented. He knew how her early life had scarred her. He understood that Lily had been unable to help herself, or change.

It was a month before a circuit judge arrived in San Juan from Santa Fe. When he did, Matt rode in alone for the trial. He gave his testimony quickly and briefly, and identified the gun that had been in Vargas' hand as he backed out the door.

The jury reached a verdict in ten minutes. The judge sentenced Vargas to hang. The date set for the hanging was April 9.

Matt returned to Two-Bar. The days and weeks fled by.

News of the war was hopeful. It appeared, from the small, grudging articles run in the San Juan paper, that the South was near collapse.

Though he did not particularly hate Vargas, Matt knew Lafferty would expect him to attend the hanging. So on the evening of April 8, Matt rode to San Juan, alone.

He arrived late at night, and took a room at the hotel. Afterward he wandered into the street and stared up at the scaffold.

He felt no qualms at the thought of watching the execution. He had seen death before. He had seen Jack Lane die and he had seen Lily die.

But it was somehow different when morning came. He stood in the bleak dawn light and watched Vargas led from the jail and along the street to where the scaffold stood.

He watched Vargas mount the steps slowly to the top, nudged on by Jaramillo from behind. He watched the man blindfolded and saw the panic in Vargas' eyes just before the blindfold covered them.

The noose was placed around Vargas' neck and tightened so that the heavy hangman's knot was on one side of his face just forward of his ear. That knot, Matt knew, was intended to break Vargas' neck as the trap beneath his feet dropped away.

Not many of San Juan's residents had turned out to watch. There were no more than a dozen standing there in the chill dawn air.

A priest from the San Juan Mission climbed the stairs and talked to Vargas briefly. Then he prayed, although Matt could understand none of the words he said. Lastly he crossed himself and slowly descended the steps.

An intolerable tension was building in Matt. He didn't want to watch but his eyes seemed glued to the man on the scaffold.

The trap fell with a crash. The rope snapped taut. . . .

Matt closed his eyes, closed out the sight of Vargas' congested face. He turned away, wanting to be sick, swallowing so that he would not make a spectacle of himself.

He did not know it then, but he found out later that while Vargas was choking on his dying breath, the Confederacy was dying too. That morning, at Appomattox Courthouse, Lee signed the surrender of his command. And a week later, Colonel Lafferty started home.

CHAPTER 7

Lafferty started home in the middle of April. But it was the last of June before he arrived.

Matt saw him coming while he was still more than a mile away. Riding a horse gaunted with the miles. Riding a horse that traveled with his head hanging wearily.

Lafferty himself was thinner than Matt had ever seen him. He still wore his cavalry colonel's uniform, though dust and mud made it look more gray than blue. His face was covered with a heavy beard. There were new lines in his face and his eyes were incredibly tired.

Matt rode out to meet him excitedly, when he recognized him, and pulled his horse to a plunging halt. Lafferty stopped too, and stared at Matt. "Matt? Good God, is it really you?"

Matt grinned foolishly, wanting to hug Lafferty. For the first time he realized how much he had changed.

He was seventeen. He had his full height if not his mature breadth. There was a stubble of light-colored whiskers on his weathered face. His eyes, blue as the sky, peered out at the world competently. He said, "It's me, Colonel Lafferty. I guess I've grown some, huh?"

"You've grown. You're not a boy any more." The colonel's voice was as tired as his face. He glanced past Matt toward the sprawling adobe house. "It looks good. It looks mighty good. How's Lily?" His eyes brightened as he spoke her name.

Lead seemed to fill Matt's chest. For a moment he didn't speak and he didn't look at Lafferty.

"I asked how Lily was." A new quality had come into the colonel's voice, a quality both tense and edgy.

"She ain't . . ." Matt's eyes suddenly met the colonel's head-on. "She's dead, Mr. Lafferty."

"My son . . . ?" For an instant something close to panic was in Lafferty's eyes.

"Nothin' wrong with him, Mr. Lafferty. He's down there at the house. He's growed some too. He's a pretty big boy now. He . . ."

He knew he was babbling. But he didn't want Lafferty to ask him how Lily died.

Lafferty stopped him with his steady glance. Matt felt his face grow red. Lafferty asked evenly, "How did she die?"

For an instant Matt did not reply. He was

trying to sort out the words he would use in his explanation. He wanted to soften it.

Colonel Lafferty's voice cracked like a whip. "How? Damn it, I want to know how she died and I want to know right now!"

"She was shot. One of the hands . . . Vargas was his name. He wasn't here when you left. He . . . he liked Lily and there was another of the hands . . ." It was a tired, sordid story, Matt realized, one with which the colonel was thoroughly familiar. He glanced uneasily at the colonel's face.

It was almost gray. And there was pain in the colonel's eyes, pain so great that just seeing it made Matt wince.

Matt scarcely heard Lafferty's voice when it came again. "What happened to Vargas?"

"He was hanged. The same day Lee surrendered for the South."

"You sure? You see him hanged?"

"Yes, sir. I watched. He's dead all right."

The colonel was silent for a long, long time. At last he said, in a voice that told Matt Lily would never be mentioned again, "Come on, Matt. Let's go home."

He kicked his tired horse in the ribs and the animal plodded down the long grade toward the house. Matt ranged alongside, holding his own prancing animal to the colonel's pace.

And now he could talk — about all the things that had happened here since the colonel left. He told the colonel how the cattle had increased. He told him how much gold was in the strongbox over at the house. What he didn't tell him was that in the last couple of months he had found the trails of several small bunches of cattle being driven off Two-Bar.

But now that Lafferty had returned . . . it would stop. Lafferty would see to it that it did.

The colonel went into the house and closed the door behind him. He reappeared in half an hour, went to the room he had formerly occupied at the end of the gallery. He gathered up his clothes and carried them over to the house. He disappeared again and did not reappear until dawn on the following day. When he did come out, Link was with him, sullen and glowering.

The uniform was gone and Lafferty wore his old range clothes. Matt never saw the uniform again.

Lafferty caught himself a horse and one for Link, who cried out in terror when he was boosted on the horse. Lafferty cursed disgustedly under his breath. The pair disappeared over the horizon and did not return until dusk.

When they did appear Link's face, though still showing his terror of the horse, also showed naked hatred whenever he looked at his father. The colonel was angry and filled with disgust. Watching Link slide off and run toward the house he said, "God! That shows you what a woman can do to a boy. He's even scared of the horse!"

Matt said, "He's only seven. He's never been on a horse before."

Lafferty snorted, "You weren't like that!" and stamped away. But in spite of his disgust, he did not give up. He and Link were together almost constantly afterward, though it was plain that neither liked the other's company.

Link grew increasingly sullen because he could do none of the things his father wanted him to do and also, perhaps, because he could not understand this violent, angry stranger whom his mother had hated and whom she had taught him to hate.

And Lafferty grew ever more impatient with Link because he could not make Link into the kind of son he wanted him to be.

Inside the tiny railroad station, the noise of the storm abated briefly, then renewed itself tenfold as hail pelted from the clouds. The hailstones bounced on the station platform, large as marbles, and from the direction of the loading pens came faintly the sounds of horses nickering frantically. Matt looked up at the clock. Almost an hour had passed, but there was still more than an hour to wait.

He paced back and forth nervously for several moments, then abruptly went over and sat down at the colonel's side. The Mexican woman's children were fussing and two of them were crying again, frightened by the racket of hailstones on the roof.

Lafferty glanced at Matt. "I've been thinking about Link."

Matt nodded. "So have I."

"I've been trying to figure out what made him like he was. That first day . . . he was even scared of the horse. I tried making a man out of him. You know how hard I tried. I wanted him to be like you."

Matt didn't reply. Nothing he could say would help.

"Hell, it seemed like he took pleasure in doing everything wrong, in making me mad at him, in making me yell and cuss at him."

The colonel stared gloomily at the floor. Matt wanted to tell him that he'd never really given Link a chance. He'd been too busy telling Link what was wrong with him, too busy trying to change him from what his mother had made of him into what he wanted him to be. He hadn't given Link a chance to respect and admire him. He'd only nurtured the hatred Lily had planted in young Link's heart. Matt doubted if Lafferty had said a single word of praise to Link in all those years.

But he didn't speak. It made no difference now. Link was what he was, what his mother, the years, and Lafferty had made of him. He could not be changed.

He had eventually learned to ride. He had learned a little cattle work. He had learned to rope and shoot. Yet it had always been plain that he learned these things reluctantly, in spite of his father rather than because of him.

Matt got up nervously. He crossed to the door of the telegrapher's office and stuck his head inside. "Train still on time?"

"Yes sir, Mr. Wyatt. They'll make it in on time too if the trestle over Big Dry Gulch holds up."

Matt closed the door. The telegraph instrument began to click busily, audible to Matt through the closed door. He began to pace again. . . .

There had been a certain excitement about the period immediately following the war. San Juan was filled with men in uniform, the uniforms of both the North and the South. It was filled with others, too, in whom the war had generated dissatisfaction with life as it had been before. Men searching for wealth. Men who were not always particular whose wealth it was.

The raids on Two-Bar cattle continued. And Lafferty was not long in discovering them. He came riding in with Link one evening and sought Matt out. "I found a trail . . . of four cattle being driven by two men. How long has this been going on?"

"A couple of months. Never any big bunches, though. Small ones — maybe two or three head. Like somebody was takin' 'em for food."

He thought Lafferty would bawl him out, but Lafferty did not. He just nodded. "We'll have to stop it. Because it won't be small bunches very long. When they find out they can get away with a few, then they're going to start taking more."

"You going to tell the sheriff in San Juan?"

Lafferty nodded briefly. Next morning, he and Link rode to San Juan. When they returned in the evening, Lafferty's eyes were cold and his jaw was set. He told Matt the sheriff had refused to do anything. He'd said he didn't have enough men to patrol Two-Bar range. Two-Bar would have to look out for itself.

And Two-Bar did. Matt would never forget the lesson Lafferty taught the countryside. He knew Lafferty wouldn't forget it either. Nor would the people of San Juan.

Immediately after his return from San Juan, Lafferty sent the hands out. "I want a fresh trail," he said shortly. "Find me one."

And he waited. With Link. With Matt. With an Indian tracker and two of the hands, one Mexican and one American.

A week passed. But at last one evening a man named Vigil came in to report the trail of about fifteen cattle being driven by four men.

Lafferty, Link, Matt, Vigil, and the other three left immediately. They rode all night and arrived at dawn at the place where Vigil had found the trail.

The Indian tracker was on it like a hound. He rode at a fast trot, all through the day. At dusk, Matt guessed the thieves couldn't be more than a dozen miles ahead. From their direction, he guessed they were heading for Albuquerque.

Again, at dawn, they were on the trail. Maintaining that fast trot that ate up the miles without tiring their horses too much.

Near noon, they sighted the dust of the cattle and drovers ahead. And now, Lafferty used some of the strategy he had learned in the war.

Vigil, along with the tracker and one of the others, was sent along the flank, told to keep out of sight and come upon the rustlers from the front. Lafferty, Matt, and the others, would come upon them from the rear. If they tried to abandon the cattle and flee, they could be cut off, no matter which way they went.

There had been excitement in it for Matt. Even now he could recall the way his hand shook holding his reins as they thundered toward the four.

The thieves had no chance to run. Cut off from flight, they sat their horses sullenly watching Lafferty and his men approach.

Lafferty rode through the bunch of cattle, reading their brands. Then he rode back to the defiant rustlers. "Shed your guns. Or use 'em. But make up your minds right now what you intend to do."

One of the four grabbed for his gun. Lafferty's gun roared once, Matt's echoing it. The man clutched his belly and tumbled off his horse.

The remaining three raised their hands. Vigil rode over to them and relieved them of their guns. With the prisoners trailing behind, Lafferty turned toward home.

Matt didn't know what he meant to do. But he had an uneasy feeling that Lafferty planned more than simply turning them over to the law. The set of Lafferty's jaw and the coldness of his eyes told Matt that.

CHAPTER 8

Lafferty led the cavalcade back toward Two-Bar, his head tipped forward, his shoulders slumped with weariness. His face, when it turned enough for Matt to see it, was brooding, almost gloomy. Exhaustion lay over it like a stain. Yet the eyes were bright, alive. They carried a touch of anger yet, though it was anger well controlled.

Behind the colonel rode Link, his young face white, his eyes holding their usual sullen, unreadable expression. Lafferty was forcing him to be a man too soon, thought Matt. Link was only eight and had seen too much violence already. Had he been left at home he would not have had to see the rustler shot. If he now had to watch a hanging too . . .

Matt shook his head impatiently. Lafferty wouldn't do that to Link. Even Lafferty wouldn't do that.

Behind Link rode the Indian tracker, whose name was Julio. His face was totally impassive and Matt wondered if he had any thoughts at all. Following Julio came the three rustlers, their hands tied behind their backs. Julio led the first horse. The second was tied to the first one's tail, and the third tied similarly to the tail of the second one.

Two of the men were middle-aged. The third was scarcely older than Matt. All three were unshaven and dirty. And all three were plainly scared. The young one kept licking his lips nervously. His knees, gripping his horse's barrel, sometimes trembled violently.

Matt followed the three rustlers, leading the horse across which the dead man lay. The rest of the Two-Bar crew brought up the rear.

Once, the young rustler turned his head and looked at Matt. He licked his lips, cleared his throat and asked, "What's he goin' to do to us?"

One of the older ones said harshly, "Shut up, Joe. Don't give the bastards no satisfaction. You wanted to go along with us. You wanted the money them cattle would of brought. Now it's time to pay up."

Panic touched the young man's eyes. Matt felt briefly sorry for him. He noticed the way the young man's knees trembled uncontrollably for a long time afterward.

They traveled steadily throughout the day. At nightfall they stopped, built a fire, and cooked the last of the trail rations they had brought along. The three prisoners were untied long enough to eat. The young one's hands shook so violently he couldn't get his coffee cup to his mouth. He finally threw it on the ground angrily. The other two stared at him with obvious disgust.

Having eaten and rested the horses, they killed the fire and mounted up again. They continued toward Two-Bar, traveling steadily throughout the night. Link slept in his saddle. Matt dozed occasionally.

As dawn began to gray the eastern sky, they rode in through the courtyard gate. The men dismounted wearily. Link stumbled toward the house, still half asleep.

It would happen now, thought Matt. Whatever the colonel intended to do would be done right now.

But he was wrong. Lafferty swung from his horse stiffly and handed the reins to Matt. "Put those three under guard. Have someone bury the other one. Then get some sleep."

He stalked toward the house, following Link. He went inside and closed the door.

Matt supervised the placing of the prisoners in one of the rooms opening off the long gallery. He saw to it they were fed, then placed a guard on the door, a man who had not been along on the chase and who therefore could stay awake. A couple of others got shovels and led the horse bearing the dead man out through the gate.

Matt walked wearily to his room at the end of the gallery, the one formerly occupied by Lafferty. He sat down on the edge of the bed and stared blankly at the door.

It was difficult for him to think. His mind was numb and his legs and arms felt like lead. Maybe Lafferty did intend to turn the rustlers over to the law, he thought. Then he shook his head doubtfully.

He leaned over and removed his boots. He unbuckled his gun belt and hung it on the bedpost. He withdrew the gun from its holster and punched the empty out, then reloaded the empty chamber.

He had shot a man, he thought, but the knowledge brought him no particular feeling of regret. Maybe he was getting calloused too. Maybe he was getting like Lafferty. Maybe, like Link, he had seen too much violence too soon.

He lay back on the bed without removing his clothes. He'd sleep an hour or so. He didn't dare sleep longer than that. He wanted to be awake when Lafferty awoke.

He seemed to be floating. The room and the bed whirled dizzily. Even if he was awake, he could not change Lafferty, he re-

alized. Lafferty was immovable, unchange-
able. Whatever he decided to do, he did.
Besides, if Lafferty had intended to hang the
rustlers, he would have done it immediately.

Relieved, he fell asleep. But it was not an
easy sleep. He tossed, and sweated, and
sometimes cried out incoherently. He saw a
huge old cottonwood in his dreams, with
three ropes hanging from a gnarled, hori-
zontal limb. He saw three horses beneath
the limb, and three men with nooses around
their necks.

He awoke with a violent start, clammy
and cold with sweat. The room was dark.

For several moments he lay absolutely
still, staring into the darkness above his
head, separating in his mind the horror of
his dream from the reality of awakening. He
felt a vast relief that the dream had only
been a dream.

Suddenly he sat bolt upright. He swung
his legs over the side of the bed and reached
frantically for his boots. He yanked them on
and groped for his gun and belt. Standing,
he belted it around him and stumbled
toward the door.

A glance told him the guard he had placed
over the prisoners was gone. He ran along
the gallery and yanked open the door of the

room he had left them in.

The room was empty. He glanced toward the house and saw that its windows were dark. It must be very late, he thought, as he turned and ran for the courtyard gate.

A single light burned in one of the adobe houses occupied by the members of the crew and their families. He hammered on the door.

It opened and a man stood framed in it, the man Matt had assigned to guard the prisoners. Matt said hoarsely, "Where are they?"

"The colonel took 'em to town."

"How long ago?"

"Two-three hours, I guess."

"Is he going to turn them over to the law?"

"He didn't say what he was going to do."

"How many men did he take?" There was a sinking feeling in Matt's midsection.

"All he could find — except me."

Matt whirled and ran for the corral, cursing softly beneath his breath. He reached it, found a rope, and caught himself a horse. He bridled him, then threw on blanket and saddle, the first ones that he found. He mounted and yanked the horse's head around toward town. He sank his spurs furiously. He thundered away through the night toward San Juan.

He knew now what Lafferty intended to do. Lafferty wouldn't have been satisfied by hanging the three rustlers where he'd caught them yesterday. He wouldn't have been satisfied by hanging them at Two-Bar when he got back. The only thing that would satisfy him was hanging them in the plaza at San Juan — where the town and everyone in it could see for themselves the terrible vengeance exacted by Two-Bar against all who stole from them.

Only that could explain Lafferty's taking the entire crew. If he'd meant to turn the men over to the law, a couple of men would have been enough.

Furthermore, Lafferty had guessed that Matt would not approve, and so had left him behind to avoid an argument.

Matt held his horse to a steady lope until the animal began to falter. Reluctantly he slowed him to a trot. He held his pace until the horse had cooled somewhat, then lifted him to the steady lope again.

Alternately trotting and loping, he covered the distance to San Juan in a little less than five hours. But the ride had never seemed longer to him. The miles seemed to drag maddeningly.

Dawn grayed the sky. The few high, scattered clouds turned pink, then orange. At last, the rim of the sun poked up above the eastern horizon, casting long shadows along the dewy ground.

Matt entered the town at a gallop, scattering chickens, pigs, and people as he rode through the narrow, alley-like streets. He rounded the corner of Domingo Street and Third and yanked his horse to a sudden halt to avoid running down members of the crowd that had gathered in the plaza.

Lafferty had used his two hour lead to good advantage, Matt saw. Two stout cottonwood posts had been set in the ground near the center of the plaza close to the bandstand. Across the top, lashed with rawhide, was a third cottonwood post. Three horses stood beneath the makeshift scaffold and three ropes with nooses were around the necks of the three rustlers.

Around the scaffold Two-Bar's riders were formed into a rough circle, facing toward the crowd. All held rifles in their hands.

Matt knew instantly that he had arrived too late. Too late to reason with Colonel Lafferty. Too late to stop what was happening. He forced his horse forward and the crowd gave way sullenly before him.

Lafferty, looking undersized and almost

ridiculous on the ground, walked stiffly to his saddle and took down a quirt. He walked back to where the three horses stood.

Matt heard the young rustler's voice, rising as he spoke until it ended almost as a scream, "Please! For the love of God, don't kill me! Please! Please . . . !"

Matt bawled, "Wait! Damn . . . !"

Lafferty turned his head. He saw Matt desperately trying to force his horse through the crowd but he made no sign of recognition. He turned his back.

He had been too far away for Matt to see his expression. But Matt knew what it was like. Like it had been the day he faced Jack Lane. Cold. Intent. Determined, almost fanatical.

The quirt slashed out. One of the horses bolted, the one on which the young rustler sat. He was yanked back over the horse's rump. The scaffold squeaked and strained.

His body hit the end of the rope but the impact did not break his neck. He hung there, kicking violently, straining to get his hands free from their bonds. His choking was audible even to Matt — audible even over the sudden, hushed sound of two hundred throats drawing in quick breaths of shock.

The quirt slashed out again and a second

horse bolted through the crowd. A second man swung beside the first.

Lafferty's quirt slashed out a third time and the third horse plunged away. And now all three bodies hung from the straining scaffold, swinging, turning on their ropes.

Matt's stomach felt empty, cold. His body was clammy with sudden sweat.

A murmur of anger came from the watching crowd. Matt suddenly sank his spurs.

His horse plunged forward, knocking men down, shouldering others roughly aside. Hands tore at Matt's legs and fell away.

Clear of the crowd, through it at last, he thundered across the small plaza, toward the scaffold in its center. His hand fumbled in his pocket for his knife.

Lafferty saw him coming and ran toward him. Reaching up, Lafferty seized the headstall of his bridle.

He was yanked off his feet by the horse's momentum but he did not let go. Matt pulled a foot out of the stirrup, put it against Lafferty's back and pushed.

The horse's head was pulled helplessly around. He lost his footing and plunged forward, throwing Matt clear to land on shoulder and back on the dusty ground.

The fall knocked the breath out of him and for several moments he lay there helplessly, gagging, gasping, trying to fill his lungs.

He got to his knees and stared at the three bodies swinging from the scaffold. It was too late now to cut them down. All three were dead.

He struggled to his feet, still fighting desperately for breath. He stared at Lafferty accusingly. "You didn't have to hang them here. You didn't have to hang them at all. You could have . . ."

"What? What could I have done? Turned them over to the law?" He laughed shortly, bitterly. "And what kind of trial would they have gotten here? Half the people in this town have been eating Two-Bar beef. But maybe they'll quit it now. Maybe when they know the price of it they won't like it so goddam well."

Matt felt like vomiting. His horse was up, shaking the dust from himself. Matt stared at the colonel's face.

The hanging had been brutal. But it had also been a challenge, thrown into the teeth of the people of San Juan. It would do what the colonel said it would; it would stop the rustling. But it would do other things as well. It would bring reprisals from the law.

Matt walked to his horse and mounted. The colonel followed suit. He led his men out of town at a deliberate walk, through the crowd which parted sullenly and into the narrow streets beyond. Behind Lafferty and his crew the three bodies turned slowly at the ends of their ropes, their boots only a foot above the ground.

Matt turned his face away. He stared at Lafferty's broad back ahead of him.

Lafferty had been different since he came back from the war, Matt thought. He had always been strong but he had never been ruthless before. Not like this at least. His face had showed no concern, no regret, no pity back there. It had been calm and cold. It had showed no more emotion than it might have shown after he'd shot a wolf.

They reached the edge of town and headed north across the grass toward home. Behind them, like thunder on a distant horizon, the voices of the outraged people of San Juan arose. In anger, in protest against the grisly spectacle in the plaza of their town — against the arrogance of the man who had put it there.

The lines of battle had been plainly drawn. The challenge had been thrown down. The struggle between Lafferty and the law would now begin.

CHAPTER 9

All morning the cavalcade bore steadily toward home. There was little talk among the men, and no exuberance. A pall of uneasiness seemed to hang over all of them. They sensed, as Matt did, that this was only the first battle of a war.

Lafferty rode at the head of the column, ignoring his men, or seeming to at least. His head sank forward on his chest. His eyes were brooding and unblinking as they stared at the empty land ahead.

Watching him, Matt felt a small chill run along his spine, as though he sensed the colonel's thoughts, as though their incredible ambition had somehow communicated itself to him.

It was nearing noon when they rode through the courtyard gate at Two-Bar ranch. Lafferty turned his head and spoke shortly to his men. "Take the rest of the day off. You've earned it. But stick around. We may have company."

He dismounted stiffly, wearily. He had won a battle, yet his face showed no elation. It was gray, moody, depressed.

Matt swung off his horse, took Lafferty's reins from him and led both horses out through the gate to the corral. He unsaddled them and turned them loose. He plodded back toward the house.

Lafferty was waiting for him. Link had come outside and now stood on the gallery watching his father with his empty, unreadable eyes. Matt felt a touch of uneasiness. Link's eyes were not the eyes of an eight-year-old. They were too wise, too old, too filled with disillusionment. The boy was a little old man, he thought. Yet there was more than age in Link's young eyes. There was another quality.

Matt frowned faintly to himself as he watched the boy. He couldn't help thinking that his own childhood had been more brutal than Link's. Why, then, should Link be so different than he himself had been?

Lafferty said, "All right, Matt. Say whatever it is you've got to say."

The old feeling of closeness with this man returned to Matt. At times like this Lafferty seemed like the father he'd never had. He said, "The sheriff isn't going to let you get away with this. He can't."

"I know. That's why I told the men to stick around."

"What are you going to do when he does show up?"

The faintest of smiles touched the colonel's mouth. "Remind him that I asked him to stop the rustling. Remind him that he told me I'd have to take care of it myself."

"He didn't mean you were to hang them in the plaza in San Juan."

"Maybe not."

"Maybe not nothin'. You know he didn't mean that. He meant for you to bring 'em in and he'd take care of them." Matt felt puzzled at himself, at his own strong feelings, feelings that seemed to have come over him suddenly. He'd never thought much about law before. Yet now he was convinced that, in order to become strong in a lawless land, the law needed the support of everyone.

His own earliest memory was of the brutal, unavenged murder of his parents. He remembered the attempted theft of Lafferty's horse, and the killing that followed it. He remembered the duel between Lafferty and Jack Lane right on Two-Bar. And he knew, suddenly, that without law to restrain them, men became savages.

Lafferty said patiently, "This ain't an easy place to live. You know that as well as me. You been fighting ever since you were a little kid. And it's worse now than it ever was. San Juan is full of human wolves. I could have turned those three over to the law and they'd have been tried. But how about the jury, Matt? Do you think they'd have found a jury that would have convicted them? Half the jurymen would probably have been rustlers themselves. They'd have turned those three rustlers loose."

Matt kicked out savagely at a rock. He stared furiously at Lafferty. The man had a way of twisting around the things he said, of justifying himself when there was no justification for what he'd done. Maybe the rustlers wouldn't have been convicted for their crime. Maybe San Juan was a lawless town. But it wouldn't be made less lawless by discrediting the law.

Matt said slowly, trying to control his anger, "There's more to this than getting rid of some rustlers. There's more to it than making an example of them."

Lafferty peered at him, his eyes suddenly very sharp. "Go on."

Matt felt suddenly at a loss, too inarticulate to say exactly what he felt. Yet in spite of his inability to express himself, he thought he knew what was driving Lafferty, and in what direction the compulsion would push the man.

Lafferty missed the war. He missed the

excitement, the conflict, the deadly challenge of it. Perhaps he even missed the violence and the brutality, which stripped a man down to bare essentials and showed him to the world for what he was. But most of all he missed the power he'd enjoyed.

Lily's death . . . the manner of her death . . . a son grown sullen and filled with hate . . . these things depressed him, and filled him with a feeling of personal failure and hopelessness. Taking on the law, throwing this brutal challenge down, had been his way of giving his life meaning and excitement once more.

Matt said harshly, "If you win . . . if you destroy the law . . . then you're going to have to take its place."

Lafferty's eyes gleamed with sudden respect. "You know me pretty well, don't you Matt?"

Matt said honestly, "I don't know. I don't really think I do." He turned and walked away, frowning, troubled by a deep uneasiness. Lafferty *had* challenged the law. That fact could not be changed. Now he would have to follow through. He didn't dare surrender himself to the hostile town and he'd probably get away with it this time. The law in San Juan wasn't yet strong enough to take Two-Bar on.

But how about the next time? And the time after that? Law would become stronger as time went on, but Lafferty's respect for it would not increase proportionally. Having challenged it once successfully, it would be easier for him to challenge it again. Until at last the time came when Lafferty and the law locked horns in a struggle to the death. When that time came, Matt knew it would be Lafferty who was destroyed.

He went to his room, sat down on the bed, and stared gloomily into the courtyard. Perhaps he was making too much of this, he thought. Perhaps he was reading intentions in Lafferty's mind that simply weren't there. Maybe this would blow over and be forgotten.

Sometimes he got up and paced the floor. Sometimes he stretched out and tried to sleep. But his tenseness, his nervous dread did not disappear.

Most of the men felt the same way he did, he thought, as he stared out into the sun-washed courtyard. They lounged in the shade of the wall, or on the gallery. Their faces were sober. Their eyes lifted often to scan the horizon in the direction of town. They cleaned and checked their guns repeatedly.

It was almost sundown when one of them

shouted suddenly, "Colonel! Matt! They're comin' now!"

Matt went out into the courtyard. He stared at the approaching cloud of dust. Lafferty came from the house and stood spread-legged on the gallery, looking like a small, determined Napoleon. Matt crossed to him and took a position at his side. Lafferty might be wrong, but that didn't change Matt's stubborn loyalty.

Lafferty turned his head and looked at him long and hard. Matt felt embarrassed and confused. Then Lafferty roared, "Get out of sight, but keep your rifles ready."

The cloud of dust came closer, and eventually resolved itself into a group of galloping men. Matt counted them. There were eleven.

The sheriff led them, a slender, dark man of Spanish ancestry. In through the gate he came and the posse galloped after him, to draw their plunging horses to a halt in the center of the courtyard.

Jaramillo was the sheriff's name, Matt remembered. Raphael Jaramillo. There was both sternness and toughness in his face, but there was no certainty. It seemed to Matt as though he knew what faced him here, as though he knew he could not succeed. He nodded at Lafferty and at Matt and said, *"Buenos tardes, señores."*

Lafferty nodded briefly. Jaramillo fumbled in his pocket and brought a folded paper out. "I have a warrant . . ."

Lafferty interrupted, his voice as cold as ice. "For what, Jaramillo? For doing your work for you? I came into San Juan and told you rustlers were working on me. Do you remember what you said?"

Jaramillo could not continue to meet Lafferty's eyes. He lowered his glance to the paper in his hand. He did not speak.

Lafferty said insistently, "Do you remember? You're damned right you do. You told me I'd have to take care of it myself. You told me you didn't have men enough to patrol Two-Bar. Well, damn you, I've taken care of it myself. And I'll go on taking care of it."

Jaramillo raised his eyes. They held cold anger now. "You have insulted me and the law I represent. You have insulted every law-abiding citizen of this county. And you did it deliberately, señor."

Lafferty shrugged elaborately. For the first time in his life, Matt was ashamed of him. Because every word the sheriff had said was true.

The sheriff unfolded the paper with trembling fingers. He read it, his English sounding stilted as he did. It charged Lafferty with the murder of three rustlers, listing their names.

Lafferty said contemptuously, "Put it away or tear it up. If you try to take me you won't leave this courtyard alive." He looked around and raised his voice to a shout, "Come on out! Show yourselves!"

Rifles poked from windows and doors. Several men appeared on the roof of the house, also holding rifles.

The sheriff's hand hung tensed over his holstered gun. He seemed about to snatch it out, then changed his mind and turned his head to look at the faces of his men.

Matt had been watching them all the time. He knew what would happen when Jaramillo turned to face Lafferty again. He'd quit. He had no other choice. The ten men with him had lost their courage and would not back him up. He might have the personal courage to fight it out with Lafferty but he wasn't stupid. He wasn't foolish enough to try it by himself.

But his eyes blazed at Lafferty. "You will regret this, señor. You cannot fight the law. The time will come when you will need the law."

Lafferty didn't reply. He stared steadily at Jaramillo until the man's shoulders slumped, until he restored the warrant to his pocket. Jaramillo turned his horse and rode deliberately through the cluster of possemen behind him. Without looking back, he went through the gate and headed for San Juan. His men followed silently.

Matt felt sorry for Jaramillo because he was finished as sheriff. He was finished because the people of the county, while they might be outraged by Lafferty's actions, were not ready to start a war with him. Jaramillo would resign. He had too much pride, Matt was sure, to continue in his job.

Matt turned and stared at Lafferty angrily. "You won," he said. "You won, but you lost too. You'll keep the rustlers off your back but is it worth the enemies you've made?"

He turned and strode angrily away. Part of his anger was directed at Lafferty. Part of it was directed at the men of Jaramillo's posse, who had lacked courage and so had let him down. But another part of it was directed at himself because he wasn't sure.

In one respect, Lafferty had been right. A trial of the three rustlers in San Juan *would* have been a farce. They'd have been released, probably without spending a single day in jail. They wouldn't have paid more than a token fine.

And if that had happened, then Lafferty would have been overwhelmed. The rustling would have become ten times worse than it had ever been before.

He also knew that had Lafferty allowed Jaramillo to take him in, he'd have been hanged for murder or imprisoned for life. Two-Bar, without him, would have been looted and destroyed.

He conceded that the law was not yet strong enough. Lafferty was right in principle, perhaps, but in practice he was wrong.

Yet he still smoldered over the arrogance of the triple hanging in the plaza at San Juan. He knew the people of the county would smolder too. Lafferty had made enemies today that would destroy him in the end.

CHAPTER 10

Matt stared gloomily out of the window of the tiny railroad station. The rain had not abated, though lightning no longer flashed so close at hand. The center of the storm had drifted farther west.

This was the culmination of Lafferty's first clash with the law, he realized. This was the end he had feared, the final challenge, the ultimate. This was the battle Lafferty couldn't win. Because this time he was challenging the law of the United States and all its awesome power would be brought to bear against him.

He found himself wishing Lafferty had failed in that bluff so many years before. He wished Jaramillo had been stronger, that his support from his posse had been more courageous. Perhaps, if it had, Two-Bar would have disintegrated. Lafferty might have gone to prison. But that wouldn't have been as bad as things were going to be when the train got in.

Doubt hadn't been apparent in Lafferty that day when he'd faced Jaramillo and his posse in the courtyard at Two-Bar ranch.

Doubt was not apparent in him now. But there must have been doubt before and there must be some now, well hidden behind his impassive, arrogant exterior.

Even if it had not been apparent in his appearance, it had showed itself in his actions after the incident. Because he set out almost at once to strengthen himself for future clashes with the law.

Jaramillo resigned as sheriff within a week. A new man was appointed to fill the vacancy, a man called Spahn.

Spahn, a stolid, thickset, hard-faced man in his fifties, rode out to Two-Bar on the day of his appointment and he came alone. He did not dismount, but when Lafferty came out, he said, "The court has withdrawn the warrant, Lafferty. It won't be served. Only don't let it go to your head. I'm not Jaramillo. If I'm sent to take you, I'll do it differently than Jaramillo did. I'll bring you in, even if I have to bring you in dead."

Lafferty nodded, without speaking. Spahn turned and rode out toward town.

Lafferty spent the day in the house. Matt did not see him at all. But the next day he came out, saddled a horse, and rode north toward Santa Fe.

He was gone for a couple of weeks. And once again the wagons began to arrive at

Two-Bar ranch. Wagons loaded with new furniture, with carpets, with dishes, and silverware. Men began riding in, announcing to Matt that they had been hired by Lafferty in Santa Fe. Some were cowhands — nothing more. But some of them were a new, hard-eyed breed who wore their guns low against their sides, who looked as though they would be very capable with them.

Nor were these the only new arrivals at Two-Bar ranch. Driving out from San Juan came others, cooks for the house, Chinese serving boys, all of whom announced they had been hired by Lafferty.

Lafferty himself returned, not riding a horse the way he had when he left, but driving a buggy rented at the livery stable in San Juan. And he brought with him a type of man Matt had never seen before, pale, elderly men in business suits who, for days afterward, drove with him across Two-Bar's scattered miles of range in the rented buggy.

Lafferty returned them to San Juan and came back again, this time riding his horse. He told Matt the men in business suits had been bankers from Santa Fe and that he'd borrowed money from them to expand Two-Bar.

Expand it he did. Up in the high country,

where timber grew straight and tall, he started a crew of men cutting logs. Not long afterward, freight wagons arrived with a huge sawmill, powered by steam from an enormous boiler. It took one of the largest wagons Matt had ever seen to transport the unwieldy thing. A planing mill came next. And not long after that wagons began hauling finished lumber out of the high country, to San Juan, to Two-Bar, even to Santa Fe, far beyond the mountains to the north.

New buildings began to go up at Two-Bar. There were new barns, a new bunkhouse for the single men, new houses for the married ones and their families.

A year passed, and a million board feet of lumber jolted out of the mountains on the rutted road. The second year, two million feet poured forth. The third year, there was a marble quarry not far from where the sawmill was and there were three new mills, each located near a particularly rich stand of timber for economy.

Matt supervised but one phase of the ranch operations now, the cattle. Lafferty was gone much of the time — in Santa Fe, in St. Louis, in Denver, or San Francisco.

But when he was back, Two-Bar hummed with activity. Buggies arrived from San Juan carrying well-dressed women and men, and the lamps burned late in the big house that Lafferty had so long ago built for his wife. There was music, provided by musicians brought in for each occasion. There was an abundance of liquor and food.

And some of the visitors were important ones. The Governor of the Territory of New Mexico. Members of the legislature. Judges, even members of the Congress of the United States.

Young Link began to grow like a weed in spring. At twelve, he was as tall as Lafferty, but thin and stringy as a bean. At thirteen, he was two inches taller than his father was.

Sometimes he rode with Matt, silent and uncommunicative. Sometimes he went on trips with his father. Sometimes he disappeared for days on end and on his return would say he had been at one of the sawmills or at the marble quarry. Or just riding the hours and days away on the vast acres his father claimed.

Lafferty had long since given up trying to change Link. He had stopped trying to teach him anything. He avoided Link, just as Link avoided him. But suddenly, now, he decided Link should go to school. Probably, Matt thought, he did so because he realized that with its growth, Two-Bar was becoming more complex. He was going to need men to handle the business details that went along with its increasing complexity. He probably hoped Link could fill this need.

So Link moved into San Juan to go to school. He was taken in by buckboard, along with a small carpetbag filled with his meager belongings. His father was not even present to tell him good-by. He was installed in a private home belonging to a widow named Willoughby, who had four children of her own. He started school.

Matt could imagine how hard it was on him. He must have keenly felt his ignorance, must have been humiliated at being forced to learn along with children half his age.

He had been gone several weeks before Lafferty sought Matt out and said, "Go on into town and see how he's getting on. Take some money and if he needs anything, get it for him."

Matt caught a horse and headed for San Juan. It was dark and overcast. He had not gone more than half a dozen miles before it began to rain.

The rain was light, soft, and warm, more of a mist than a rain. Low clouds hid the peaks to the north and drifted across the rock faces of an occasional mesa which broke the flatness of Two-Bar range.

He kept his horse at a steady trot along the rutted, heavily traveled road. He passed three freight wagons hauling lumber before he reached the outskirts of the town and stopped briefly to talk to each of the three teamsters.

San Juan had changed much since the triple hanging several years before but this was the first time Matt had visited it since then. It was bigger. There were dozens of new adobe houses. There was a big, new three story hotel facing the plaza. There was a new bandstand where the old one had formerly stood and there was grass in the plaza where previously there had been only hard-packed earth.

Matt halted his horse at the edge of the plaza and stared at the spot where Lafferty's scaffold had stood. All the old memories came back to him, the horror, the chill, the anger. Impatiently he turned away, turned his back both on the scene and on the memories it invoked.

It was just after noon and the rain had stopped. It took him a while to find the school, which he had never seen before.

It was a fairly new frame building, no doubt built with lumber from the Two-Bar mills. Unpainted, it sat on the edge of town a couple of hundred yards from the San

Juan River. On three sides of it were crowded run-down adobe shacks.

Matt halted his horse at the edge of the cluster of shacks and stared at the schoolyard, in which there were almost a hundred children of all ages. Many of them were Mexican.

He sat there for a long, long time, trying to locate Link. At last he centered his gaze on a group at the far edge of the schoolyard close to the riverbank.

Link must be one of those, he thought. He headed his horse toward them, but on an impulse not immediately clear, circled and came up on them from the direction of the river bed.

Screened by brush and by the river bed itself, he halted. He could see Link now. He stood in the center of a circle formed by yelling boys, facing another about the same size as he.

All the boys were yelling taunts. As Matt watched they began to chant, "Ya, ya, Link Lafferty! His old man's a bastard, and so is he!"

Link launched himself at the boy facing him. He was awkward and gangling and most of his blows went wild. The two fell and grappled on the ground. For a few moments they were hidden from Matt's view by the circle of onlookers.

From the schoolhouse came the jangling of the bell. Matt glanced that way and saw a woman on the schoolhouse porch ringing it. Children began to stream reluctantly toward the sound.

The group around the two combatants thinned and disappeared among the others heading toward the schoolhouse. But Link remained. So did the boy who was straddling him, beating him with his fists.

Matt touched his horse's sides with his heels. He rode deliberately toward the pair, understanding that Link would not want him to actively interfere, understanding also that when Link's antagonist saw him coming, he would get up and leave.

Seeing him, the boy glowered at him briefly. Then, with a final, deliberate punch into Link's unprotected face, he got up and swaggered toward the school, looking back over his shoulder at Matt defiantly.

Matt got down from his horse. Link got to his feet, knuckling tears and dirt from his eyes. Matt said, "Hello, Link."

Link glared at him silently. There were smudges of dirt on his face and streaks where the tears had run across his cheeks. There was blood on his mouth and one of his eyes looked as though it might turn black.

But there were other marks on his face that had not been made today. Matt asked, "You do this often?"

Link glanced up at him sullenly, and as sullenly glanced away. He did not reply. Matt said, "The colonel sent me in to see how you were getting along."

Link growled, "He can go to hell!"

Matt felt irritation stir in him. "That fight wasn't the colonel's fault."

Link met his glance and his eyes were furious. "That's all you know! That kid's pa was one of the men he hung in the plaza when he first came home."

"And you've fought him before?"

Link stared at him pityingly.

"Do you always get the worst of it?"

Without looking at Matt, Link growled, "Some day I won't get the worst of it no more. I'll kill the sonsabitches, that's what I'll do!"

In that instant he looked like Matt imagined the colonel might have looked at the age of thirteen in similar circumstances.

Link said sullenly, "I got to go in."

"Sure. You need anything?"

Link shook his head.

Matt shrugged. "All right. Go on."

Link hesitated a moment. It was as though he wanted something from Matt, something he could neither define nor understand. Then he turned and shuffled toward the schoolhouse.

Frowning, Matt watched him go. His own childhood was not so long gone but what he could remember the terror he had known during the Comanche attack in which his parents had been killed. He could remember being alone at the burned-out Texas ranch until Lafferty had come. He could remember his paralyzing fear when the men from the trading post tried to steal Lafferty's stallion. And there had been plenty of other times when he'd been scared.

So he knew how Link must feel, alone, alien among all these hostile kids. Neither at home nor here could Link find approval. Only criticism and dislike. And not for anything he had done or failed to do. Only secondhand hatred directed toward him instead of toward his father where it belonged.

But he was his father's son, whether the colonel approved of him or not. He wasn't running away. He was standing and fighting against overwhelming odds, every day.

Matt frowned as he rode away from the school, puzzling as to why Link fought. He wasn't fighting for Lafferty. He wasn't really fighting for anything and it would have been easier for him to run. What Link was doing, Matt decided, was fighting *against* things because he was so filled with hate.

A sudden parallel struck him suddenly. Lily had fought the way Link now fought, blindly and with hatred against everything and everybody who made her feel cheap or inadequate. She had never fought *for* anything either. She had always fought against things because she hated them. Two-Bar, Lafferty, the people of the country who had snubbed and ignored her. Her fighting had taken a different form than Link's because she was a woman, but it was otherwise the same. She fought to hurt, and even her drunkenness, her men had been parts of the fight.

Matt took the road toward home. The sky was clearing now and the sun beat down warmly upon the steaming land.

How would he explain Link to Lafferty, he wondered, when he had difficulty understanding Link himself? How could he tell the colonel that Link needed him when he couldn't tell him why in terms the colonel would understand?

For a moment, he wondered what would happen to Link when he was grown. If he went on hating everything, if his hatred didn't die somewhere along the way, there could be but one end for him. Men didn't fight with their fists the way boys did. They fought with guns.

He arrived at Two-Bar at dusk. But when he faced Lafferty's questioning eyes and his words, "How is he?" he could only answer noncommittally, "All right, I guess," and let it go at that. There was too much confusion in his own mind about Link to explain the boy to Lafferty.

But he did realize that ultimately Link was going to have to take sides. He must either stand on his father's side or on the side of his enemies. Hating both his father and the people of San Juan, it would be a difficult choice for him to make. But if he went on fighting both Two-Bar and those who hated it, he would only succeed in destroying himself.

CHAPTER 11

Matt was gone from the home place for about a week afterward. During that time, Link gradually faded from his mind because he had decided there was nothing he could do about the boy.

He arrived back home late. The setting sun bathed the land with its orange-colored, dying glow.

Matt sat for a moment, staring at the ranch, thinking how much it had changed in the few short years since Lafferty had returned. It looked almost like a town, a town dominated by the sprawling adobe ranch house.

Freight wagons loaded high with lumber and slabs of marble were drawn up in a line outside the courtyard gate. The corrals, covering five or six acres, were filled with milling draft and saddle horses. Men moved around in the compound formed by buildings and corrals. Smoke rose from half a hundred chimneys as the supper hour approached.

Matt rode in, put his horse in one of the corrals, and lugged his saddle and bridle toward the house. He put them down on the gallery as Lafferty came out of the house and bawled, "Matt!"

Matt walked along the gallery toward him. Lafferty seemed excited. "Come on in, Matt. I want to tell you what I'm going to do!"

Matt followed him into the house. Lamps were burning here and there. Matt accepted a cigar from Lafferty and lighted it.

Lafferty said, "I'm going to build a slaughterhouse and packing plant."

For a moment, Matt didn't reply. He stared at Lafferty in amazement. At last he said, "Won't that cost a lot?"

Lafferty nodded. "The money's no problem. We've paid back the loans on the sawmills and marble quarry. We're making money hand over fist. Now, by God, we'll get big — really big."

Matt asked, "Why?"

For an instant Lafferty stared at him. "Why?" he roared. "I'll tell you why! Because we can't stand still. People like to tear big things down and Two-Bar is the biggest thing around." He seemed a little confused, suddenly, and turned abruptly to stride to the window.

Matt didn't point out the inconsistency of what Lafferty had said. He knew it would be no use. Besides, he knew the answer. Lafferty, because of his small stature, felt compelled to prove himself over and over again. He wouldn't stop. He wouldn't rest until Two-Bar was as big as he could make it.

Napoleon, whom he resembled, must have felt the same compulsion, thought Matt. He had gone on and on, conquering, adding to his empire. Until at last he overextended himself. Until he met defeat.

Lafferty turned and looked at him, something almost pleading in his glance. Matt asked, "Where's the slaughterhouse and packing plant going to be?"

"At the mouth of Soda Canyon." Lafferty looked expectantly at him.

Matt nodded. It was the logical place, he realized. The canyon was deep where Soda Creek cut through on its way south across the plain. The canyon mouth, for about a mile, was sheltered from the sun except when it was high at midday.

There was a wide spot in the valley, wide enough for buildings and corrals. There was water. And there was a place where a dam could be thrown across the creek to form an ice pond behind it.

He said, "It's a good idea."

For a moment Lafferty seemed disappointed in him. Then, his own enthusiasm took hold of him. He talked steadily for more than an hour.

The next day, he headed for Chicago. And once more the wagons began to arrive, this time from the east, bringing heavy machinery and endless cases of cans. Men began to arrive, too, men Lafferty had hired in Chicago, men who knew the packing-house business.

In one respect, Matt realized, Lafferty did things right. When he entered a new venture, one with which he was unfamiliar, he hired men to run it that knew how.

And so, the packing plant and cannery rose in the mouth of Soda Canyon. And the cattle on Two-Bar, instead of trailing north toward Albuquerque and Santa Fe, streamed instead into the gaping mouth of the Two-Bar slaughterhouse and emerged, neatly canned, ready to be hauled off northward and eastward toward the end of track. Soda Creek turned red, and the stench of the packing plant, if the wind was right, reached all the way to the house and the veritable town of buildings that surrounded it. But it was the smell of money and no one seemed to mind.

Another new venture was started at Two-Bar the following year. Two-Bar began to raise horses for Army remounts, from mares brought up from Mexico and from stallions supplied on loan from the U.S. Army itself.

Matt didn't like the slaughterhouse and cannery. He didn't like the sawmills and marble quarry. Matt liked the cattle business, and he spent most of his time these days riding across the endless miles of Two-Bar range in the company of the Spanish and Anglo cowboys, many of whom had worked for Two-Bar a long time ago while Lafferty was away at the war. He spent his nights in line cabins, and he saw little of Lafferty.

An empire was growing here on the New Mexico plain, he realized. But it was an empire of which he wanted no part. It was an empire that excluded him, that crowded him away from its pulsing heart.

It was also an empire that, as time went on, required its own police force, and this was another part of it that Matt didn't like.

Several hundred men now worked on the ranch — at the three sawmills, at the marble quarry, at the packing plant. Half a hundred more worked with the cattle and the Army remounts.

Quarrels were inevitable. And since Lafferty refused to call on the law, it was up to him to maintain order himself.

The necessity of it was impressed on him about a year after the packing house began turning out canned beef.

Even now, that incident was brutally clear in Matt's memory. He had been at home when word came of the trouble and Lafferty had been there too.

A man came riding in about dusk, hatless, on a horse that was lathered and faltering. He pounded into the courtyard yelling, "Colonel! Colonel Lafferty!"

Matt came out onto the gallery as Lafferty emerged from the house. School was out for the summer and Link, still-faced and sullen, stood in the doorway behind his father.

The man tumbled off his horse. "There's trouble at the cannery! Al Lake says you'd better get the sheriff and a posse and get there as quick as you can. He'll try to keep 'em from doing anything until you do."

Lafferty said, "Whoa now. What the hell are you talking about?"

"It's the men, Colonel. They been trying to get Al to raise their pay."

"Why haven't I heard anything about it?"

"Al didn't want to bother you. He thought he could handle it."

Matt didn't recognize the man. He obviously didn't work in the slaughterhouse. One of the office workers, Matt supposed.

"What are they doing? What's this all about?"

"They struck, Colonel. They quit work about the middle of the afternoon. Al fired the whole bunch of them when they refused to go back to work."

"He did right."

"Maybe, Colonel. But it didn't work out so good. They got mad when he fired 'em. They began tearing things up. Al and a couple of others got guns. They shot three men. Two of them are dead. The others holed up in the hide shed. Al's trying to keep them there but he figures as soon as it gets dark, they'll get out. He figures they'll burn the whole damned place."

Lafferty looked across the courtyard at Matt. He roared, "Get some men, Matt! Get 'em quick!"

Matt ran across the courtyard and out the gate. He yanked his revolver and fired a couple of shots into the air.

Men poured out of the bunkhouse and out of the houses that had been built for the married men and their families. He yelled, "Get mounted! I want at least a dozen of you!"

He ran toward the corrals. He snatched a rope from a nail on one of the corral poles and went inside. He began to rope horses.

Julio, the Indian tracker, Vigil, and a couple of others came in and began to help. Matt bridled two horses and led them at a run toward the house. He saddled them, finishing as Lafferty came running across the yard, buckling on his gun.

Lafferty mounted and Matt followed suit. They spurred out of the courtyard and headed for the corral.

Half a dozen men were already mounted. Others were working as fast as they could, catching horses and saddling. Lafferty turned north toward the packing plant, spurring his horse into a hard run. Matt followed, fifty feet behind.

The others strung out for a half mile behind. The light was fading rapidly and it would soon be dark. Even riding this way, they could not possibly reach the mouth of Soda Canyon until an hour and a half after dark. By then the damage would be done. Unless Al Lake somehow managed to keep the rebellious workers holed up in the hide shed.

However hard he spurred his horse, Matt could not catch up with Lafferty. The man rode as though possessed. Matt could imagine what his face looked like. It would be grim, intent. Probably almost calm. Lafferty's eyes would show his anger, though. They would be blazing with it.

Halfway to Soda Canyon, Lafferty was forced to slow his horse. Matt continued at the same speed until he caught up. The others began straggling up behind until all were riding in a group.

Matt didn't ask Lafferty what he was going to do. He didn't have to ask. Lafferty would do whatever had to be done to protect the packing plant. Men would be dead before this night was through. More than the two Al Lake had shot.

Lafferty walked his horse for half a mile. Then he spurred him into a steady lope. The men kept pace.

It was completely dark. Matt began to strain his eyes ahead, in the direction of the packing plant. He would see a glow in that direction, he thought, if the workers managed to escape from the hide shed, if they managed to set fire to anything.

They were only a couple of miles away when Matt first saw the glow. It was visible on the ridge beyond the packing plant. It outlined the mouth of the canyon in sharp relief.

And then Matt heard shots, sporadic, widely scattered shots, as though someone were sniping at men only occasionally exposed.

Lafferty, Matt, and the others pounded into the canyon mouth. They thundered along the road that led to the loading dock. Lafferty pulled his horse to a halt in the center of the jumble of buildings, staring first at the blazing hide shed, then toward the cannery, then toward the slaughter-house. From the direction of the corrals came the uneasy bawling of cattle. Lafferty bawled, "Al!"

"Here, Colonel Lafferty!" The voice came from the loading dock, from behind cases of canned meat awaiting removal to-morrow.

Lafferty rode to the dock. He asked, "Where are they now?"

"I been holding them behind the hide shed. They don't dare run out for fear I'll cut 'em down. But as soon as it burns out . . ."

Lafferty turned his head and looked at Matt. "Take half the men and go to the left of it. I'll take the rest around to the right."

Matt didn't need any more instructions than that. He knew what Lafferty wanted done, knew what had to be done.

He headed across the clearing. The group of men split, half going with Matt, half with Lafferty. Matt's horse avoided the two bodies lying on the ground fifty feet from the dock, shying at the sight of them.

The stench of the place was in the air, thick, cloying, sweetish, and sickening. Matt wondered how men lived, breathing a stench like this every hour of every day.

Lafferty yelled and Matt sank spurs into his horse's sides. The animal leaped ahead, and behind Matt the others forced their horses into a run, keeping pace.

Gun in hand, Matt rounded the blazing hide shed. He saw the faces of the men turned toward him. He heard a shot, and felt the buzz of a bullet past his cheek.

Suddenly, behind them, Lafferty opened up. The man who had fired at Matt straightened violently as the bullet took him in the back. He twisted sideways and collapsed silently to the ground.

Another man, a half-naked giant of a man, whirled to face Lafferty. He held a cleaver in his hand.

His muscles bulged as he drew back his arm for a throw. They gleamed with sweat in the firelight.

Matt's gun was in his hand. He needed no time to draw, only time to swing the muzzle toward the man and thumb the hammer back. He knew where that cleaver would go when it left the giant's hand. It would go straight at Lafferty and split his skull. . . .

He fired instantly. The man seemed to stiffen. Matt fired again. No time now for a third shot. The man's bulging arm flung forward and the cleaver left his hand, turning over and over in the air, catching the red gleam of the fire and throwing it back every time it did.

Matt opened his mouth to yell at Lafferty. Then he saw that the cleaver was falling short of where Lafferty sat his horse.

He switched his glance back to the man who had thrown it. There was red on the man's back now. He was staggering.

He collapsed suddenly, face downward on the ground. Lafferty roared, "Hold it, every goddamn one of you! Throw your weapons down!"

The fight was gone from them. One by one their guns, their knives, their hastily snatched weapons thudded to the ground. Lafferty bawled, "Now get buckets, by God, and put that fire out before it spreads!"

Dazedly they shuffled away. Dazedly they began to fight the blaze. Matt turned his head and shouted at his mounted men, "Get off your horses and give them a hand!"

They dismounted and hurried to help fight the blaze. Lafferty's half dozen men followed suit. Matt rode to Lafferty. "What are you going to do to them?"

Lafferty said, "I'm going to raise their pay. That's what they want, isn't it?" He grinned at Matt suddenly. "What the hell did you expect me to do, string 'em up?"

Matt stared at him puzzledly for a moment. Then he swung from his horse and went to help fight the fire, which had, by now, nearly consumed the hide shed. Scowling angrily, he thought he would never understand Lafferty. Never in a thousand years.

Nor did he understand any better when Lafferty hired Les Saxon and put him in charge of a mobile band of private police, to handle future occurrences similar to the strike at the packing plant.

The months dragged past and sometimes it seemed to Matt as though he were drawing further and further away from Lafferty with every passing month.

Fortunately, there was no test of strength over the dead at Two-Bar's packing plant. Their deaths were listed as justifiable homicide since they were engaged in rioting and destroying property at the time they had been shot.

But another, more deadly contest developed out of it. The families of these four dead men joined with the families of the three hanged rustlers. And once more Lafferty had to fight for the survival of the empire he had built.

CHAPTER 12

It was a different kind of battle that developed now. It was a kind of battle Lafferty had never fought before. But it was also one for which he had, intentionally or not, equipped himself.

The first indication that it had started came when Spahn, sheriff of San Juan County, came riding in at Two-Bar one afternoon with a paper issued by the District Court in San Juan. It directed Lafferty to show cause why the land he claimed should not be thrown open to homesteading under the Homestead Act of 1863.

Lafferty accepted the paper silently. He watched Spahn ride out, his mouth twisting wryly at the satisfied expression Spahn's face had worn.

Matt asked worriedly, "Can they make that stick? What kind of title do you have to all this land?"

"Part of it is an old Spanish Grant. That's the part the house sits on. It isn't a big grant, as Spanish land grants go, but it's around a hundred thousand acres. I bought it from the descendants of the original owner when we first came here. I paid twenty-five cents an acre for it and I just finished paying up a year ago."

"What about the rest of it?"

Lafferty frowned. "Most of it still belongs to the government. I've pre-empted some of it — the sawmill sites, the marble quarry, and the mouth of Soda Canyon. But they can hurt me just the same if they make this stick. Hitch up a buggy, Matt. I think we'll just go up to Santa Fe and see what can be done."

Matt hitched up a buggy and packed a small valise. He and Lafferty drove north.

It took them five days to reach Santa Fe. They were days of pure pleasure for Matt. Again it was as it had been so long ago when Matt had ridden up from Texas behind Lafferty on the big black stallion.

In Santa Fe, however, Lafferty virtually disappeared. He would leave the hotel in early morning and would not return until late at night. Matt wandered through the narrow, crooked streets, marveling at the ancient buildings and churches, drinking in the small cantinas, eating Spanish food in the cafes or just sitting on a bench in the plaza across from the hotel.

For the first three days, Lafferty would return to the hotel room late at night, his face worried, a perpetual scowl on his forehead. But on the fourth day, he returned looking satisfied. He dragged out a bottle of whiskey and poured both Matt and himself a drink.

Matt said, "You look as if you'd done some good."

"Maybe I have, Matt. Maybe I have. The governor is going to Washington next week. He knows a lot of influential congressmen and senators. He's going to try and get a bill introduced — as a rider on another bill. If we're lucky, it'll slide through without being noticed. And it will give me title to Two-Bar that nobody can contest."

"How'd you manage that?"

Lafferty grinned. "It took some doing, Matt. It sure as hell took some doing."

Matt could imagine the kind of doing. He wondered how much money Lafferty had passed around as bribes.

"It wasn't all bribery, Matt," Lafferty said, as though sensing his thoughts. "I did some talking, too. I convinced 'em that Two-Bar would bring millions into this territory. I convinced 'em that if they let it be destroyed they'd ruin the economy of the territory, that they'd set back our chances of being a state by twenty years." He stared at Matt intently. "I believe that, Matt. I honestly believe it's true."

Matt studied him. Tonight, he saw in Lafferty a rueful kind of apology. He saw the colonel's need to justify whatever it was that he had done.

Lafferty poured himself another drink and gulped it down. He filled his glass again and stared at it gloomily. At last he said, "This ain't my kind of fighting, Matt. They smile at you and shake your hand but you know it's deadly just the same. You dance with their women and drink their whiskey. And it's when they're the nicest to you that you have to be most careful." He gulped his whiskey and shook himself noticeably. He seemed to be shaking off his own feeling of distaste and guilt. "Well hell, it's done anyway. We can go home and forget about it."

"What if the bill doesn't get passed?"

"It'll get passed, Matt. It'll get passed. But I hope I never have to fight this way again."

Matt laid awake for a long time, staring toward the low ceiling of the room. Lafferty tossed uneasily in the other bed.

For the first time in his life, Matt wondered what his own future was. Would he remain with Lafferty, supporting him in each new battle that he fought, until he was old himself? Or would he leave, and lose himself someplace where no one had ever heard either of Lafferty or Two-Bar ranch? Would he find a woman he wanted, and marry her, and raise a family of his own?

Why was he so fiercely loyal to Lafferty? he asked himself. Was it because Lafferty had saved his life many years before on the brushy Texas plain? Was it because Lafferty was the closest thing to a father he had ever known?

He didn't know. He didn't suppose he would ever know. He fell asleep finally, but it was not an easy sleep. It was tormented by dreams. Uneasy dreams, of Lafferty and Link and of the triple hanging years before. He awoke next morning with an uneasy memory of his dreams.

They drove back south in the buggy, making the trip this time in four days instead of five. And Matt went back to riding, to working with the cattle, staying away from the ranch house as much as possible. And while the questions he had asked himself in Santa Fe did not torment him continually, they remained in his mind, unanswered.

Through an attorney in San Juan, Lafferty obtained delay after delay on the show-cause order of the court. Until at last, nearly a year after the buggy trip to Santa Fe, he received title to Two-Bar in a way that could never be questioned again. The bill had been passed by the Congress of the United States. The rider attached to it had been passed along with the bill. To the original hundred thousand acres contained in the Spanish Land Grant had been added half a million more.

All of Lafferty's troubles did not come from forces outside the ranch. Link continued to confuse and puzzle him.

At sixteen, Link was almost as tall as Matt. And though he no longer went to school, rarely now was Link at home. When he was, he avoided Lafferty.

Lafferty's answer to personal failure had always been the same. It was no different now. He threw himself into the work at Two-Bar, rising before dawn each day, staying away from the ranch house until long after dark. He wore out two or three horses every day, and his own face began to grow gaunted and thin with weariness.

Matt, though he did not see the colonel often, did not miss the change in him. Each time he saw Lafferty his own expression became more worried, his own mouth more grim.

The colonel needed him now, he realized, as never before in his life. The colonel needed someone who was close to him to discuss his trouble with. And no one was close to Colonel Lafferty. No one was close to him but Matt.

Knowing he would never bring the subject up himself, Matt brought it up. Encountering Lafferty spurring recklessly across the plain one day, Matt asked deliberately, "Something's worrying you, isn't it?"

"No more now than ever, Matt."

"It's Link, isn't it?"

Lafferty stared at him with sharpened eyes. For a moment Matt thought he would spur his horse and thunder away, but he did not. He remained silent for a long, long time and at last he nodded almost reluctantly. "Yeah, Matt. It's Link."

He got heavily from his horse. He began to pace restlessly back and forth. Without looking at Matt, he said, "I don't understand him, Matt. I can't. It's like he'd closed a door someplace and I can't get through to him."

"Has he said anything? Or done anything?"

"Not to me. He never says anything to me. He just grunts at me. He was always gone a lot, but I always knew he was on Two-Bar someplace. Now he spends his time in town. He's drunk damn near every day. Sometimes he comes home all beat up and I can't even get him to tell me what the fight was about."

Matt didn't speak. There was nothing he could say. Yet he understood that just by listening to Lafferty he was helping all he could. Link was a problem Lafferty himself would have to solve — if the problem could be solved.

Lafferty turned suddenly and stared up at him. He asked, almost angrily, "Do you hate me, Matt?"

Matt stared at him in amazement. "Hate you? Why the hell should I hate you? You picked me up down in Texas when I would have died if you hadn't come along. You . . ."

He didn't finish because he could see Lafferty wasn't listening. Lafferty asked, "Then why should Link hate me?"

It was a while before Matt answered him. He was thinking, remembering many things. Lily for one. She had planted poison in Link's young mind from the time he had been old enough to understand.

Lafferty hadn't helped things when he returned after the war. He'd given Link no reason to like him. He'd given the boy no chance to understand him. Link probably understood Lafferty even less than the colonel understood his son.

Lafferty was watching him expectantly and Matt knew he had to give him an answer of some kind. Maybe he'd get pulled off his horse and punched in the mouth for his pains but he had to try. He said, "It ain't only one thing. It's a lot of things. Lily for one. She poisoned Link while you were away in the war. She taught him to hate you like she hated you."

"But I've tried to . . ." Lafferty shook his head helplessly.

Stiffening himself, Matt asked, "Have you? Link didn't measure up to what you thought he ought to be and you tried to change him the way you'd break a horse. Maybe it would have worked if he hadn't been taught to hate you before you started it. But he had and he was scared of you."

Lafferty glared at him and for a moment Matt wondered if he would yank him off his horse for what he'd said. But Lafferty did not.

Matt went on, "Link has been alone ever since he was born. Lily was too busy drinking and chasing men to bother with him. He saw her killed and that must have

147

scared hell out of him. Then when you came back — Colonel, Link was scared of you too. He was along when we caught those rustlers. He saw one of them killed. He saw your face and he heard about the hanging in San Juan. When you sent him to school he had to fight somebody damn near every day. It's a wonder he ain't a lot worse than he is."

Lafferty stared at him pleadingly. "What am I going to do? I can't talk to him. It's like talking to a damn stone wall."

Matt said, "I can't do any better, but I'll try if you want me to. Maybe he was so young . . . maybe he doesn't know what his mother really was or why she taught him to hate you like she did."

The look of gratitude on Lafferty's face embarrassed him, and he regretted his promise almost as soon as it was made. What could he do with Link that Lafferty couldn't do? What could he tell the boy that would make any difference to him?

His own feelings toward Lafferty were mixed. He admired the colonel, but he saw the weakness in him too — the weakness of pride, the everlasting sensitiveness about his size, and the need to prove himself. He was grateful to Lafferty but there was more to it than gratitude. The plain truth of the matter was that he worshiped Lafferty. The colonel had become, to him, the father he had never known. He knew he would die unhesitatingly for Lafferty if there was ever need for it. He knew he would back Lafferty, and stand with him, no matter what the colonel did.

He also knew he could not, with words, communicate this feeling about the man to Link. But he could try.

Lafferty mounted and rode away. Matt rode toward the house to talk to Link.

CHAPTER 13

Link was not at the house when Matt arrived. No one seemed to know where he was.

Matt hadn't really expected to find him at home. Judging by what Lafferty had said, Link spent most of his time in town. But he'd come back. Drunk and sick and often beaten up, he'd come home. So Matt stayed at the home ranch, waiting for him.

Link did not return that day. Nor did he return the next. Lafferty came back and, as the hours passed, his expression grew worried. At last he sought Matt out and said, "Let's go in to town, Matt. Something might have happened to him."

Matt didn't believe it had. But there was no sense in arguing. He saddled up and rode out with the colonel just after noon.

Lafferty's face was drawn. And today, Matt noticed something he had never noticed before. Lafferty was showing signs of age. His hair, around the temples, was getting gray. His face was lined, more so than ever before. His eyes had lost their zest, their reckless challenge.

He swung around in his saddle as they left

the buildings of Two-Bar and stared behind. The place was bigger than San Juan had been when the two of them first came here. It was busier too.

And he realized something else about Colonel Lafferty, something he had never really considered before. Lafferty had built an empire here in the empty reaches of New Mexico. He had amassed a fortune. But he had made no friends. He still, after all these years, had no one upon whom he could depend — no one who understood him or even tried — no one but Matt.

Lafferty glanced at him and, with an insight that surprised Matt, said, "I've done everything I set out to do. I've built Two-Bar into what I wanted it to be. But it seems like nothing. It seems like nothing at all."

Matt nodded. He stared at Lafferty's tortured face and knew the colonel was thinking of Lily and of Link.

He felt a sudden touch of anger. Lafferty was a good man, in his way. Ruthless perhaps. Even brutal sometimes. But not with his family. He had been good to Lily and he'd tried to be good to Link.

He felt his throat tighten up and felt a burning behind his eyes. He wanted to say, "It isn't all bad. You've got me and I'll never let you down."

But he didn't say it. He wasn't, after all, a member of Lafferty's family. He was only a waif Lafferty had found and raised.

They reached San Juan in late afternoon. The town seemed to have prospered in recent years. There were many new buildings that appeared to have been built in the last year or two. There was a new residential section of two- and three-story houses, all of which were new. A well-to-do section, Matt thought. A section from which most of Lafferty's opposition came.

There shouldn't be much of that any more. Not active opposition at least. Lafferty's title to Two-Bar was secure. They couldn't attack it and it was doubtful if Lafferty would challenge the law again the way he once had done. Perhaps, thought Matt, the peace that had come to Two-Bar was part of the colonel's trouble, and responsible for his depressed state of mind. Lafferty needed something to fight, something to pit himself against, and there wasn't anything left for him to fight.

He asked, "You want to go with me? Or do you want me to dig him out?"

Lafferty hesitated and it was not like him to hesitate. At last he said, "You dig him out, Matt. If you need help, I'll be in the hotel bar."

Matt nodded and watched him ride across the plaza. He watched him dismount, noting how heavily he tramped across the walk and into the hotel.

He crossed the plaza himself, dismounted, and entered one of the saloons. He crossed to the bar and ordered himself a beer. He turned and let his glance run over the occupants of the room.

Link wasn't here. Unless he was upstairs.

He sipped his beer thoughtfully. There were probably a couple of dozen saloons in San Juan. He might not find Link at all. Link might be sleeping it off in an adobe shack someplace.

He finished the beer and went out. He walked along the plaza to the next saloon and went inside. He looked around, but he did not order anything.

Doggedly, he covered all the saloons in the central part of town, without success. He headed into the Spanish section.

He found Link in the third place he visited. It was a tiny place, set back from the street, with a small, dirt-paved courtyard. Link was sleeping at a table, an empty bottle in front of him.

Matt stood looking down at him. Link's hair was long and untidy. He had not shaved for at least a week. His clothes reeked.

Matt pulled out a chair and sat down. He had promised Lafferty that he would talk to Link. But first he'd have to sober him up.

He said, "Link."

Link didn't stir. Matt reached out and touched Link's shoulder. He shook the boy gently and said, "Link, wake up."

Link raised his head. His eyes were bloodshot and narrowed against the light. His mouth was slack and he was drooling from one corner of it. He did not immediately recognize Matt. When he did, he scowled and muttered, "Go away. Lemme alone."

"Uh-uh. You come along with me. We'll get some coffee and something to eat."

Link dropped his head down onto the table again.

Matt shook him again. Link raised his head. He took a clumsy swing at Matt across the table, a swing Matt avoided easily. But the bottle crashed to the floor.

Matt got up. He went around behind Link and hoisted him bodily to his feet. Link began to curse him sourly.

He half carried, half dragged Link from the saloon. Outside, Link pulled angrily away. He staggered and nearly fell. He stood, spread-legged in the courtyard, weaving back and forth. He cursed Matt steadily.

Matt stepped close to him and slapped him on the side of the face. "Shut up. You're going with me, whether you like it or not."

Link took another clumsy swing at him and missed. Matt closed with him and began once more to drag him along.

He took Link into a small restaurant a block from the plaza. He ordered coffee for him and watched him drink it. After three cups, Link seemed to be a little more sober.

Matt said, "The colonel wanted me to talk to you."

"I got nothin' to say to you."

"Well, I've got a couple of things to say to you. Come on." He got up. Link remained where he was, so Matt yanked him to his feet and shoved him toward the door.

Link went out. He was walking steadily now and the back of his neck was a deep brick-red. Matt said, "You're a bum. I don't know why the hell I bother with you."

Link turned and glowered at him. "Because you want Two-Bar, that's why. Because you'll do any goddam thing he tells you to get your hands on it."

Matt said wearily, "Go on."

"All right, I will! If he'd been home like he should've been, she'd still be alive. But he wasn't home. He was off playing soldier, getting himself called colonel."

"His being gone didn't have anything to do with it."

"You're a liar!"

"You really believe that, don't you?"

"Damn right I do. I know it. The son-of-a-bitch!"

Matt doubted if Link really did believe what he claimed to believe. It was just something his mind had invented to make the fact that he hated his father easier for him to accept. But it was time Link knew the truth.

Matt said, "You were pretty young so maybe you don't know. But it's time you did. Your mother was a slut. She took up with every man that came along. She was killed by one of the men she was finished with."

Link's face turned gray. He stared at Matt with eyes that were wild with fury. But there was sickness in his eyes as well, behind the burning rage.

Matt said brutally, "Lafferty got her out of a saloon in Albuquerque. He built her a big new house. He tried to make a lady out of her but he never could. She was a bum from the day he found her until the day she died."

Link backed slowly away from Matt. There was shock in his eyes. His face was

156

twisted and his lips were almost white. He muttered, "Liar! You filthy liar!"

Matt knew suddenly that he had gone too far. He had not meant to be so brutal about it. Now he saw what Link intended to do. Link was going to force him into a gunfight. Right here. Right now.

He said, "Link . . ."

Link was now twenty feet away. His hand, hanging close to the grip of his gun, was trembling violently. Matt felt a little sick. He couldn't draw against Link. Link was shaky and still unsteady from the liquor he had consumed. If he shot Link, even in self-defense, the colonel would kill him like he would a wolf.

Yet if he didn't draw, if he didn't defend himself, Link was going to kill him. In another ten or fifteen seconds, Link was going to draw. Maybe he wouldn't get Matt with his first shot, but he had five bullets in his gun. He'd get Matt with one of them.

For what seemed an eternity, Matt stood there motionless. His mind was racing, seeking some way out.

Link's voice was almost a scream, "Draw, damn you! Draw!"

Matt's hand snaked toward his gun. Link grabbed his frantically and yanked it out. He fired instantly as it came up.

Matt dived sideways, falling, rolling in the dusty street. Link's gun blasted a second time. The bullet showered Matt with dirt.

He steadied himself for an instant, and in that instant flung his gun at Link. It struck Link full in the chest, driving a gusty grunt from him.

Link fired again. This bullet ripped into Matt's thigh and he felt the instant rush of blood.

But he was up, driving toward Link, half crawling, half running, trying to cover the twenty feet separating them before Link could shoot again.

The fourth shot blasted almost in his ear and he felt the bullet graze the long muscles lying along his spine. Then his shoulder struck Link, knocking him back a full half dozen feet before he spilled into the dirt.

Matt was on him like a mountain lion. His hand groped for Link's gun, found it, and wrenched savagely.

The gun blasted a fifth time, almost in his face. The acrid bite of powder smoke stung his lungs. But he had the gun and now he flung it halfway across the narrow street.

Link fought like a bobcat, whimpering and sobbing with effort and frustration as he did. There was a roaring in Matt's ears. There was a burn like fire along his back and in his thigh. His head reeled and he could feel weakness overcoming him.

If he passed out . . . Link would recover one of the guns and kill him where he lay. He knew that more certainly than he had ever known anything.

He seized Link by the throat. He began to bang Link's head methodically against the ground.

Hands seized him from behind, hands with an incredible strength to them. He was yanked away from Link and flung backward into the dust.

He slumped against an adobe building wall. He stared.

Lafferty was helping Link to his feet. Link jerked away from him and lunged for Matt's gun. He got his hands on it but the colonel was too quick for him. He kicked it savagely out of his hand.

Link stood up. His face was dusty and his eyes were crazy wild. Lafferty cuffed him angrily on the side of the face. "Get out of here! Go home!"

Matt didn't know, for a moment, if Link would obey or not. Then, with a last smoldering glance at the two of them, he turned and shuffled sullenly away.

Lafferty turned and glared at Matt. "I said talk to him, not kill him."

Matt said, "Damn you, he emptied his gun at me. If I'd wanted to kill him he'd be lying there right now."

Lafferty picked up Matt's gun. He glanced down at it and spun the cylinder. He tossed it to Matt, who caught it and holstered it.

Lafferty picked Link's gun up. He spun the cylinder of it too. He thrust it into his belt.

He crossed to Matt and helped him to his feet. The back of Matt's shirt was drenched with blood and so was his trouser leg. Lafferty asked, "Can you walk?"

Matt nodded irritably and took a step toward where his horse was tied.

He felt himself falling, felt the impact of the ground. The world turned black and for an instant he felt as though he were whirling crazily. Then he knew no more.

CHAPTER 14

Inside the railroad station the Mexican woman's children were sleeping now. And outside, the rain had all but stopped. The land around the station lay wallowing in mud. The lightning-struck tree smoldered, sending up a thin blue plume of smoke. In the corral behind the station the horses stood dispiritedly.

Overhead, clouds still scudded along on a high wind. Plumes of low-flying cloud sometimes hid the mesa tops, but here and there patches of blue were briefly visible, and here and there a ray of brilliant sunlight would occasionally stream through to touch the land lightly before disappearing again. At least, thought Matt, they wouldn't have to fight in a drenching rain.

He found himself thinking of Laura. The fight with Link had been responsible for his meeting her, and for that, he supposed, he should be grateful to Link.

He awakened that day in a pleasant room with whitewashed walls and curtains at the window. He was in a bed. His clothes had been removed and bandages were wound around his chest, others around his thigh.

It was quiet in the room and for a while he lay staring at the window, remembering the fight, remembering the way he had passed out. He must have lost a lot of blood, he thought, for he still felt weak, drained of all his strength.

He lay there, awake, for almost an hour before he heard the door open. Turning his head he saw a dark-skinned man in middle age and a young woman in a white dress that almost touched the floor.

The man crossed to the bed and picked up Matt's wrist. The woman stood a few feet behind him, her face turning pink under Matt's steady scrutiny.

Dropping Matt's wrist, the man said, "I'm Dr. Chavez and this is Laura Peabody. How do you feel?"

"Weak." He became conscious of his nakedness beneath the blanket and suddenly found it difficult to meet the young woman's eyes. His own face flushed and her eyes twinkled when it did.

Dr. Chavez said, "Miss Peabody wants to be a nurse." He stared at Matt for several moments, then asked, "Do you want something to eat?"

Matt nodded, and asked, "Where's Colonel Lafferty?"

"He went home. Something about his son. He said you were to stay here until you were strong enough to come home."

"When will that be?"

The doctor permitted himself a spare smile. "You're young and strong. A week, perhaps."

He turned and left the room. Laura Peabody came over to the bed and straightened the blankets. Matt held onto them fiercely. The mocking light in her eyes taunted him. She said, "Don't be so modest, Mr. Wyatt. I helped the doctor bandage you."

She stood looking down at him for a moment, her smile slowly fading. "You were lucky, Mr. Wyatt. You could have been killed."

He didn't reply. She turned and left the room, closing the door quietly behind her.

Matt tried, almost desperately, to remember her, to fix her in his mind. The white dress, he recalled, had failed to conceal the straight, slim lines of her body. Her hair had been drawn back severely from her face and tied in a bun at the back of her head. Her eyes had been blue, a rather startling blue, and they had been warm and filled with laughter. Her mouth had been full and smiling.

He had never met a woman like her

before. His contacts with women had been limited to Lily, and to the wives and daughters of the Spanish vaqueros at Two-Bar.

She was gone about half an hour. When she returned, she carried a tray. While she arranged it on a table beside the bed, Matt sat up, wincing with the sharp pain in his back and leg as he moved.

Laura Peabody pulled up a chair and watched him while he ate. When he had finished, he asked, "Have you lived in San Juan long?"

"Since I was ten." Her face was suddenly almost expressionless. "Colonel Lafferty hanged my uncle in the plaza eight years ago. My father came here afterward and decided to stay. He sent for my mother and me."

Matt said, "I'm sorry."

She smiled faintly. "I never knew my uncle. And besides, you have nothing to be sorry for. You tried to stop it."

Matt stared at her in surprise. "How did you know that?"

Her mouth held a touch of bitterness, as did her voice. "I know every detail of that hanging. I've heard my father go over and over it, a thousand times, I guess."

"I expect he hates the colonel quite a bit."

She nodded, the bitterness remaining in

her eyes. "Can't we talk about something else?"

"Tell me about yourself."

She smiled. "I went to Santa Fe to school. I guess it was there that I decided I wanted to be a nurse. We read about the Crimean War and about Florence Nightingale. . . ." She talked on, softly. For a while, Matt listened, but gradually drowsiness came over him. He closed his eyes. . . .

He smiled to himself, now, as he thought back on it. Something had been between Laura and himself from the very first. She had spent a lot more time with him than had been required. And when, after a week, he got up, dressed and headed back to Two-Bar, he told her he would call on her.

She wouldn't let him call on her. Not at her home. She said her father would never permit her to know anyone connected with Two-Bar ranch. But she would meet him beside the San Juan River, a quarter mile from town.

He saw her regularly, twice a week, all that summer and well into the fall. But he had known, almost from the first, that he wanted Laura, wanted to marry her.

It was in October that it all came to a sudden end. He was sitting with Laura on the riverbank, staring at the shine of the moon on the narrow stream, talking. . . .

He heard a branch crack behind him. He heard a man's deep voice saying something he did not understand. He jumped to his feet, a warning tingle touching the hairs that lay on the back of his neck.

A rifle prodded him savagely. Laura cried out with sudden fear. . . .

Then they were surrounded, by half a dozen men. He heard Laura say, "Father! What . . . ?"

And he heard Peabody's harsh voice, "Take her home, Sam."

"Father, I won't go. I love Matt and he wants to marry me."

Peabody's laugh was bitter, harsh. "Take her home, Sam."

One of the men took hold of Laura's arm. She struggled. Matt moved suddenly. His fist slammed against the man's jaw and flung him back. . . .

They were all around him in the darkness. Something struck him behind the ear. He went down and felt a savage kick in his ribs. Half stunned, he could hear Laura screaming, but her screams were fading as someone dragged her forcibly away.

He fought furiously to his feet. There was something gleefully vicious in Peabody's voice as he said, "All right, boys. She's gone now. Let's give this son-of-a-bitch something neither he nor Lafferty will forget real soon."

Matt backed toward the San Juan River. A man rushed, swinging wildly. Matt avoided the swing and the man stumbled past. Matt raised his knee and caught the man squarely in the face with it. He felt teeth give, felt the sharp pain of them biting into his knee. The man howled and fell into the river shallows with a splash.

A blow struck the side of his neck. Another smashed him squarely in the mouth. His own fists were windmilling, occasionally landing, but there were still four of them. They beat him backward, into the river shallows, and out into the stream. His lips became a pulp. His nose streamed blood. There was a knot the size of a walnut on one of his cheekbones, another on his forehead.

His right ear was torn and streaming blood. His ribs, already cracked from the kick, cracked again under their brutal blows.

He went down in the shallow water. Their boots stamped him, kicked him, in the head, in his cracked ribs, in his belly which was already sore from their blows.

Peabody yelled, "Let up! I ain't through

with the bastard yet!"

He felt hands dragging him from the river. His lungs were half filled with water and he bent double, trying to cough it out.

On the bank once more, Peabody said with soft savagery, "All right, hold him there. Just like that. I'll finish this myself."

Matt tried to raise his head. His arms were held by two of Peabody's friends. He let his weight fall heavily on them and raised both feet. He kicked out at Peabody with all his strength.

His feet caught Peabody in the groin. The man doubled and sank to his knees. Another of the men moved in.

Peabody raised his head. His face was white above his beard and his eyes glittered in the cold moonlight. In a voice tight with pain, he said, "No! I said I'd finish him!"

The men holding Matt twisted his arms cruelly. He bit his lip to keep from crying out. The only sound that came from him was a grunt.

Peabody struggled to his feet. He moved in close to Matt and said, "You filthy, dirty, son-of-a-bitch!"

Then he began to hit Matt in the face. His blows had a sodden, smacking sound because of the blood streaming from Matt's nose and mouth. Twenty — thirty — forty times they struck. Matt felt consciousness fading from his mind. But he kept his burning eyes on Peabody's face until the world turned dim. His body slumped, his whole weight now resting on the men who were holding him.

He heard Peabody's voice, as though from far away. "Dump him in the river and let's go home."

He felt his body turning over and over as it was rolled down the bank. He felt the coolness of the river and heard the splash. He heard the sounds they made crashing through the brush as they left. Then all was quiet again.

His face was in the water, but it was too shallow here to drown. He heard someone groaning but it was several minutes before he realized the sounds came from his own battered mouth.

He tried to raise himself and failed. Laboriously, an inch at a time, he began to crawl toward the riverbank.

He reached it and raised his head and chest out of the water. This way, half in the water, half out, he stayed. His eyes closed and he lost consciousness.

When he awoke, it was broad daylight. The sun beat down upon his back. He could hear some small boys talking excitedly in Spanish. He tried to open his eyes and failed. He raised a hand and discovered that both of them were swelled tightly shut.

He tried to speak, but his mouth was stuck shut with dried blood. His whole body was a mass of pain. His head ached viciously. The voices of the boys faded and there was silence once more. He lapsed into unconsciousness again.

When he awoke a second time, strong hands were lifting him. He was placed in the back of a buckboard. He heard Sheriff Spahn's voice saying, "Drive him on out to Two-Bar. Let Lafferty take care of him."

He remembered now, remembered all that had happened the night before. Laura had been dragged away. And then her father and his men had beaten him mercilessly.

The buckboard jolted away, its motion rolling Matt helplessly back and forth. His head ached ferociously, so that he found it hard to think. He wondered if Laura knew what they had done to him. He wondered what Peabody had done to her.

Through town the buckboard went, and out onto the grassy plain. Thirty miles, it was, and it would be night before the buckboard arrived, before Matt could be washed and bandaged and put to bed.

The sun climbed high in the sky and beat steadily down into Matt's face. The driver kept the team at a trot, and the jolting kept Matt's injuries hurting continuously.

Half a dozen times during that endless day, he lost consciousness. Half a dozen times he was jolted out of it by a particularly painful lurch of the buckboard in which he lay.

The sun dropped across the western sky, unseen by Matt, whose eyes still were closed. And at last, as dusk settled quietly across the land, the buckboard pulled into the courtyard at Two-Bar and stopped.

Matt heard voices, Spanish voices, English ones. He heard a door slam heavily and a few moments later heard Lafferty's booming voice, thick with anger and outrage. "What happened to him? Who did this to him?"

And the driver's voice, anxious and touched with fear, "I don't know nothin' about it, Colonel Lafferty. Some boys found him down on the bank of the San Juan early this morning. Sheriff Spahn told me to drive him out here. That's all I know."

Hands lifted Matt out and carried him to the house. Matt heard Lafferty cursing as they carried him inside.

He was stripped and laid on a bed. Gentle

hands washed his wounds. Cold compresses were put on his eyes and mouth, and changed frequently. Tight bandages were wound around his chest to support his broken ribs.

Lafferty came in while they were working on him. He said, his voice strangely gentle, "Matt?"

Matt grunted.

"Who did this to you?"

Matt grunted again. Lafferty would probably kill Peabody if he knew all that had happened last night. If that happened, Laura would be forever lost to him.

Elena, one of the women working over him, said, "He can not speak, Señor Lafferty."

He felt Lafferty's presence beside him for several moments more. Then Lafferty said, "All right, Matt. We'll talk about it tomorrow."

He went out, closing the door softly behind him. The women finished with Matt, covered him, and, except for Elena, also left. Matt, his body one steady, burning throb of pain, let himself slip into unconsciousness. His last thought was that this was one act of violence that would not beget more violence. He would never tell Lafferty who had beaten him.

CHAPTER 15

It was a week before Matt could get out of bed. For another week he hobbled around with a cane, favoring his broken ribs. Lafferty questioned him on several occasions about who had beaten him but Matt stubbornly refused to tell. He had almost made up his mind to leave Two-Bar anyway. When he was well enough, he meant to ride to San Juan, get Laura, and go away someplace. Someplace where nobody had ever heard of Colonel Lafferty and Two-Bar ranch.

He seemed to take forever to mend, but at last, two weeks after the beating, he saddled a horse, mounted and headed for San Juan. It was midafternoon when he left. He planned to arrive in San Juan after dark.

There were still evidences of the beating on his face. He still moved gingerly, favoring the broken ribs. He turned and looked back at Two-Bar once, wondering if he would ever see it again.

He felt vaguely ashamed at leaving Lafferty this way. Then he clenched his jaws and continued on toward town. Lafferty didn't need him. Lafferty had Two-Bar, and

Link, and money and power. . . .

But he didn't quite succeed in convincing himself. He knew Lafferty did need him. He was the only human being in the world that even bothered to try to understand Colonel Lafferty.

He rode steadily, feeling the rise of excitement in his mind. Laura. In a few more hours he would see her. Before nightfall they would be married. They'd go away, and forget Two-Bar. They'd forget San Juan, and her father, and the hanging so many years before.

The sun dropped behind the horizon and dusk crept across the land. In the twilight, Matt entered San Juan.

He rode along the narrow streets until he reached Dr. Chavez's place. He rode into the tiny courtyard and dismounted stiffly. He tied his horse and knocked on the heavy door.

Dr. Chavez himself answered it. Matt said, "I'm looking for Laura. Is she here?"

Chavez shook his head. He stared at Matt steadily for a moment, then said, "Come in, Matt."

Matt went inside. Chavez peered at him critically for several moments before he said, "That was quite a beating."

Matt grinned wryly. "It was." His grin

faded. "You haven't told me about Laura. Where is she? Do you know?"

"Not exactly. She's not in San Juan. Her father sent her East almost two weeks ago."

Matt stared. There was an empty feeling in him. She'd gone without seeing him, without getting word to him, without even knowing if he was alive or dead.

He found himself thinking of Lily suddenly and wondered why. Laura wasn't the least bit like Lily.

He stared at Chavez bleakly. "Didn't she even see you before she left?"

Chavez shook his head. "What happened between you two? I heard about the beating because you were hauled right through the center of town. But . . ."

Matt said, "I'd been seeing Laura. I wanted to go to her house but she wouldn't let me do that. She said her father would never allow her to see anyone that was connected with Two-Bar ranch. So we met down by the riverbank. A couple of weeks ago her father and some of his friends surprised us there. One of them hauled her away and the others beat me up. I just got out of bed yesterday. I was going to find her and marry her and take her away with me." He stared at Chavez emptily, nodded and turned heavily toward the door. Chavez said, "Maybe I could find out . . ."

Matt shook his head. "Never mind. She knows where I am and she can write. If she wants me to know where she is, she'll let me know."

He went outside and closed the door behind him. He stood there for several moments, staring bleakly into the darkness. Then he mounted and rode back toward home.

He knew what had happened. Laura had been forced to make a choice. She'd made it and that was all there was.

He felt anger beginning to stir in his mind. A man was a fool to trust a woman, he thought. Lafferty once had trusted one and she had all but ruined him.

Suddenly he sank his spurs cruelly. His horse leaped ahead and broke into a hard run. His face grim, his eyes smoldering, Matt rode him this way until he stumbled and nearly fell. Then, with sanity slowly returning to his mind, he pulled the horse to a halt.

He dismounted from the trembling animal. He stripped the saddle off and rubbed the lathered horse down with the saddle blanket.

When the horse was rested, he remounted and headed home again, riding at a walk.

His anger had cooled. He could think of Laura without resentment now. She was only a girl, after all, and he supposed he couldn't blame her too much.

But the hurt remained. It remained for a long, long time afterward.

The attempts on Lafferty's life had been, Matt supposed, inevitable from the first. Lafferty had won every skirmish with his enemies. It was to be expected that, balked in each attempt to defeat him, one or more of them would eventually seek his death, by whatever means possible.

It was early summer when the first attempt was made. Matt had just taken a herd to summer range in the high country on the north rim of Two-Bar range. He was heading back, accompanied by half a dozen of the hands, when a man came pounding toward them from the direction of the house.

He hauled his horse in, plunging, and yelled excitedly, "Matt! The colonel's been shot!"

Matt turned his head toward the nearest cowhand. "Change horses with him."

The two changed horses. Mounted on a fresh horse, the messenger kept pace as Matt and the others thundered toward home. Matt yelled, "How bad is it?"

"They got 'im in the leg. Same bullet killed his horse. He bled a lot before he was found."

Matt's breath sighed out slowly. He felt almost weak with relief. At least Lafferty was alive, and while a leg wound could be serious, particularly if there was a substantial loss of blood, Matt knew how tough Lafferty was.

He questioned the messenger as to Lafferty's condition but the man didn't know any more than he had already told. He had left to summon Matt immediately after Lafferty had been brought in.

An hour passed, and another. The horses trotted steadily, but occasionally Matt would urge them into a lope, maintaining it as long as possible before slowing them again.

It was almost ten o'clock when he arrived. He swung from his horse at the courtyard entrance with curt instructions for the men. "Saddle fresh horses and find out where the colonel was found. Locate Julio. We'll be trailing as soon as it's light tomorrow."

He walked across the courtyard fearfully. There were lamps burning in the house. The door stood open and he went inside.

Lafferty lay on a leather-covered couch in

the living room. He was covered with blankets beneath which his left leg showed bulkier than his right. Matt stared at his face, which was very pale.

Maria Chavez and Elena, the cook, were both with him. Matt asked, "How bad is it? Did the bullet hit the bone?"

Maria shook her head. "No, señor. But he lost much blood."

"Who bandaged him?"

Maria said, "I did, señor. I poured whiskey over the wound before I did. My husband has gone to bring the doctor from San Juan."

Matt nodded. He pulled a chair close to the couch and sat down. He stared into Lafferty's pale face.

Lafferty opened his eyes. He grinned weakly at Matt. Matt asked, "Did you see him, Colonel? Do you know who it was?"

Lafferty shook his head. "I heard his horse, but I never saw either him or the horse." He closed his eyes. His breathing became heavy.

Matt got up. He stared down at Lafferty worriedly. He heard a commotion in the courtyard and went outside.

A buggy had driven in, accompanied by Maria's husband, who was now dismounting from his horse. Dr. Chavez climbed out of the buggy. "Hello, Matt. Where's Colonel Lafferty?"

"In here." Matt led the way into the house. The doctor crossed to where the colonel lay. He sat down in the chair Matt had just left and picked up the colonel's wrist. Frowning slightly, he peeled back the blanket and, with scissors taken from his bag, began to cut the bandages off.

Matt paced back and forth nervously. He heard the doctor grunt something unintelligible and asked, "How bad a wound is it?"

"Missed the bone. Missed the artery too, or he'd be dead. He'll be limping around for a while, but he'll be all right."

Matt felt a vast relief. "I'll be going, then."

He started out the door. Chavez said, "When you catch him, Matt . . . give the law a chance."

Matt nodded without conviction. He went on out and walked toward the cluster of men and horses at the courtyard gate. The men who had ridden in with him were there. So was Julio, the Indian tracker. There were a couple of others besides.

Matt asked one of them, "Where was he found?"

"You know that big dead cottonwood about halfway to town?"

Matt nodded. He swung to his horse, whirled him, and rode away. The others kept pace, riding slightly behind.

He held the pace to a walk most of the time, wanting the horses to be fresh when dawn came. The hours crept slowly past.

At three in the morning, they reached the dead cottonwood. Matt dismounted and stretched out on the ground. The men followed suit.

Matt closed his eyes. He didn't have to trail the assassin to know who he was. Furthermore, he knew where the trail would lead. It would lead to San Juan. If they didn't lose it there it would lead straight to Ford Peabody's house.

He slept briefly and awakened as gray began to outline the horizon in the east. Julio was already scouting around on foot. The others, also awake, waited silently in the chill dawn air.

At last Matt heard Julio shout. He mounted and rode toward the sound. Julio handed him a brass cartridge case.

The trail followed the bed of a dry stream for about a quarter mile. Then it headed straight for town. The sun tipped the clouds with pink, then rose and climbed slowly across the sky.

Counting Julio, there were six men with

Matt. They rode silently, their faces intent. Matt remembered suddenly Dr. Chavez's words, "Let the law have a chance."

He doubted if the law could do anything. This trail would be obliterated by traffic in the town. He might know who had shot Lafferty but he'd never be able to prove it to the satisfaction of Sheriff Spahn. Ford Peabody wasn't the only one who hated Lafferty, even if his hatred did seem the most intense.

The trail continued unerringly toward San Juan. They reached the outskirts of the town.

Julio dismounted now. Matt kept the men a dozen yards behind. Julio quested through the streets like a hound, but when he reached the plaza he finally stopped. He looked back at Matt with a helpless shrug.

Matt said, "Try the streets leading away from the plaza."

Julio nodded and set off at a trot. Matt rode to where he'd left his horse, bent low and gathered up the reins.

But Julio did not pick up the trail again. And finally Matt was forced to give it up.

Scowling, he led his men to Ford Peabody's house. He took Julio into the stable at the rear of the house and had him inspect the hoofs of the two horses there. Neither was the horse they had been following.

Balked and angry, he stared at the house. He knew Peabody had been the one, but he couldn't prove it. Certainly not to Spahn's satisfaction.

Peabody came out of the house. He was unarmed and the fact that he was made a wry expression touch Matt's face. He was even more certain now.

Peabody glared at him. "What the hell are you doing here? Get out of here or I'll have the law on you."

Matt asked, "What did you do with the horse?"

"What horse? What are you talking about?" Peabody's expression was suddenly bland, no longer showing anger at an intrusion he would have considered unwarranted and arrogant had he not been hiding something.

"The horse you rode when you ambushed Lafferty." Matt stared at Peabody, hating him as he had never hated anyone in his life before. He could almost feel Peabody's fists slamming into his face that night on the riverbank. He could almost feel Peabody's boots slamming into his unprotected body.

"I don't know what the hell you're talking about. But I'm glad to hear Lafferty's been shot. I hope he's dead."

"I hate to disappoint you, but he's not."
Matt watched Peabody's face closely as he
said the words. He saw the raw fury, the
keen disappointment that crossed Peabody's face.

And suddenly his own fury blazed. Because he couldn't touch Peabody for
shooting Lafferty from ambush. He had no
evidence and the law couldn't do a thing.

He turned his head and glanced at Julio.
"Get behind him, Julio. If he tries to run,
trip him up."

Grinning, Julio jumped to a position
behind the man. The others who had come
with Matt formed a large, loose circle. Peabody swung his head frantically, looking for
escape. Matt said softly, "You ambushed
Lafferty. You beat the hell out of me while
your friends held my arms. I'm going to give
you a better chance than that, but it's going
to come out the same. If you can crawl back
in the house afterward, you'll be lucky."

Peabody was a big man, as tall as Matt
and heavier. His shoulders were wide, his
chest deep. There was gray in his hair and
his belly bulged slightly.

His face was hard, lined in such a way as
to give it a perpetual smoldering, angry
look. His eyes were blue, narrowed now and
hard.

Understanding it was to be only the two of them, he stopped looking around for a way out. A certain satisfaction came into his chilly eyes. He stood hunched, waiting.

Matt said, "If he beats me, Julio, let him go. Understand?"

Julio's grin widened. "Si, señor. But he will not beat you."

Matt moved forward carefully. He meant that this should be more than a simple fight. He meant to leave Peabody battered and unconscious when he rode away. He intended to beat Peabody as badly as the man had beaten him.

CHAPTER 16

Between Peabody and Matt, the ground was clear and level, covered with high grass and low weeds. Behind Peabody, closer to the house, there was a woodpile and chopping block. In back of Matt was the stable.

From ten feet away, Peabody put down his head and rushed. Like a maddened bull he charged toward Matt.

Matt leaped aside enough to avoid the battering ram Peabody had made of his head. But the man's arms outstretched, caught him and swept him back.

He staggered, off balance, elbowing Peabody on the side of the head as he did. Freed of the man's arms, he whirled to face him. Peabody had stopped his charge and now swung around.

Matt swung a savage fist, with all the weight of his body behind it. It smashed squarely into Peabody's face. The man's nose began to spurt blood from both nostrils and he swiped at it angrily with the back of his hand.

Matt followed instantly with a veritable rain of blows. Peabody gave ground, backing, until the stable wall stood at his back. Matt, wild with fury, swung another blow and this one, too, had all the weight of his body back of it.

Peabody ducked aside and Matt's fist slammed into the stable wall. Pain shot from the hand all the way to his shoulder. The men watching gasped sympathetically in unison.

The pain was excruciating. It made Matt's head whirl, made his stomach churn. He stood there for a moment, numbly shaking his head. Peabody seized the initiative. His fist crashed into Matt's mouth, smashing his lips against his teeth.

Matt backed warily, still shaking his head. His hand, his whole arm was numb and felt almost as though it were detached from his body. He backed across the yard, ducking some of Peabody's blows, giving ground before those he could not avoid. He backed into the woodpile and sprawled helplessly on his back.

Peabody dived at him and Matt rolled aside. He scrambled away from the woodpile and got unsteadily to his feet.

Both men were breathing hard, sucking great breaths of air into their laboring lungs. Peabody came to his feet clutching a length of firewood in his hands.

He swung it at Matt and Matt ducked under it. He swung his fist wildly and it connected solidly with Peabody's head as the man was turned involuntarily by the weight of the swinging length of firewood.

Again pain shot all the way to Matt's shoulder, but the blow slammed Peabody back and made him sprawl, as Matt had, on the pile of firewood.

Matt stepped in close. As Peabody struggled to his hands and knees, Matt kicked him savagely on the side of the head. Peabody sprawled back a second time. This time when he came stumbling to his feet, he held a double-bitted ax in his hands.

Matt backed warily. Grinning out of a bloody, battered mouth, Peabody advanced, the ax held with his right hand near the head, his left halfway up the handle. Held this way, his swing with it would be short but well controlled.

One of Matt's men yelled, "Drop it, you son-of-a-bitch!" but Matt turned his head briefly and panted, "Let it be!" He backed from Peabody steadily, wondering how he was going to get past that deadly ax to the man holding it.

He felt, rather than saw, the stable at his back. He turned his head fleetingly. The door was right behind him. There would be a pitchfork inside. . . .

Turning suddenly, he lunged, running, through the door. Peabody uttered a howl and plunged after him.

The fork was on the far side of the stable, half buried in a pile of hay. The two horses threw up their heads, snorting, and stared fearfully at the two combatants.

Matt plunged across the stable toward the pile of hay. Swiftly he glanced over his shoulder at Peabody.

The man had raised the ax. Held in but one hand now, it hung poised over his right shoulder. Matt realized he was going to throw it.

He tried to swerve, to turn, to get out of the path of the murderous thing. He saw it leave Peabody's hands and come flying toward him, turning over and over in the air.

A foot went out from under him as he stepped on the edge of the loose pile of hay. He sprawled to the floor helplessly. The ax whirled over his head.

Peabody, close behind it, tripped on his sprawled-out body and fell face downward in the hay.

The fleeting thought of what that ax would have done to him had he not fallen turned Matt weak. He clawed toward his antagonist, seeing Peabody's hands now groping for the fork.

He seized one of Peabody's feet while the man's hands were yet inches short of the fork. He tugged, slipping in the loose hay.

Peabody kicked out with the other foot. It smashed into Matt's face, flattening his nose, making tears come springing to his eyes.

But suddenly his fury became overpowering. He released Peabody's foot and drove himself above and across the man. His hands closed on the handle of the fork.

He pulled it toward himself, rolling, holding the handle close to the three-tined fork. He jabbed at Peabody furiously.

Two of the tines buried themselves in Peabody's upper thigh. His voice came out in an agonized sound of pain that was almost a scream. He rolled away frantically, trying to get out of the pitchfork's range.

Clinging to the fork, Matt made it to his feet. He stood spread-legged, panting, and stared at Peabody, who was crawling away from him frantically.

There was a red haze over Matt's eyes. A red haze of rage. Peabody had tried to kill him with the ax. He would have killed him with the fork if he'd gotten his hands on it first.

In Matt, too, was still the memory of that

night on the riverbank. Peabody had meant to kill him then. He'd left him for dead, face down in the water.

Matt had the advantage now. He could kill Peabody if he wanted to. And he did want to. Peabody was potentially a killer even if he wasn't yet a murderer in fact. He had tried to kill Matt. He had tried to kill Lafferty yesterday.

But suddenly, unbidden, came another memory. Matt's shoulders slumped, though he did not release the fork. This was Laura's father, however improbable that fact seemed.

Peabody raised himself, pulled himself up along the stable wall with his hands. His leg almost gave way under him. Matt saw blood spreading from the two holes the pitchfork tines had made.

He glanced toward the door. His men were crowded together there, peering in. Matt walked toward them wearily, still holding onto the fork. They stepped aside and he went through the door.

He flung the pitchfork angrily toward the house. The tines buried themselves in the frame wall and the pitchfork hung there, vibrating up and down with its own weight. Matt staggered toward his horse, caught up the reins, and swung heavily to the saddle.

Peabody had come to the stable door. His face was bloody and battered, his complexion gray with pain. He watched Matt and his men numbly as they turned their horses and rode out of his yard.

Matt did not look back. He felt cheated. His right hand and his whole right arm ached with steady throbs, each of which made him wince. His breathing did not become normal until long after they had left the town behind.

He had wanted to beat Peabody into unconsciousness and he had failed. But he admitted that his failure was not because of inability to do so. He had simply grown disgusted with Peabody's attempts to turn the fight into a battle to the death. And he had grown afraid of his own compulsive desire to kill the man.

Lafferty mended quickly. A month after being shot, he was getting around normally. It took almost that long for Matt's hand to heal.

But from the day Lafferty first ventured out of the house on crutches, Matt stayed virtually glued to his side. He knew the depths of Peabody's hatred of Lafferty. He knew Peabody would try again, and again, until either he or Lafferty was dead.

The days and weeks fled past. In late October, on a day when chill wind blew down off the high peaks to the north, Peabody's second attempt was made.

A couple of men recently hired brought Lafferty the news that they had cut the trail of rustlers. A bunch of forty or fifty head, they said, being driven by two men. Lafferty and Matt saddled up and, taking the two men who had brought the news, rode to intercept the rustlers.

Matt wondered at the increasing uneasiness in the two as they approached the spot where the pair had cut the trail. It could simply be fear of the coming encounter, he thought. But it could also be something else. He dropped back until he was behind the pair. And he began to watch them more carefully than he did either the trail or the country ahead.

The shot came unexpectedly, from the lip of a dry wash a hundred yards to the right of the trail they were following. Just before the shot came, however, Lafferty's horse shied violently from something he had seen in the wash. The bullet missed.

Lafferty's spurs sank instantly in his horse's sides. He reined the plunging animal right and thundered along the bottom of the wash toward the spot from which the shot had come.

Matt, still short of the wash by forty or fifty feet, also sank his spurs. He pounded toward the shooter too, gun in hand. The two who had drawn them here with their story of rustling, fled the other way, forcing their horses into a steady run.

Matt glimpsed Peabody's horse before he saw the man himself. But as he neared the lip of the wash, he saw Peabody running toward the horse, a rifle in his hand.

Recklessly, Matt plunged his horse directly over the edge of the wash. The horse squealed with terror as he fought for footing. Matt sank spurs furiously, righted the horse with an inflexible hand on the reins, then plunged him directly at the running man.

The horse's chest struck Peabody, knocking him forward, skidding on his face. The rifle left Peabody's hand. The horse's plunging feet kicked him as the animal went over the prostrate man.

Lafferty, coming up behind Matt, hit the ground running. A stunned Peabody yanked his revolver out. Lafferty kicked it out of his hand.

The hammer of Lafferty's revolver was back, the gun pointing at the man on the ground. Matt opened his mouth to yell, then shut it suddenly. If ever a man had justification for killing another, Lafferty had it now.

But Lafferty didn't shoot. He holstered his gun and looked up at Matt. "You been telling me to give the law a chance. All right, let's see what the law does with this."

Peabody got up, shaken, bruised, white of face. He limped to his horse as though fearing Lafferty might change his mind. He climbed to the saddle and looked at Matt.

Matt said, "All right. Head for town."

Peabody led out, with Matt and Lafferty following him.

They did not reach town until late that night. Even the jail was dark, but a few minutes after Matt started pounding on the door, a light flickered inside and the door opened.

Spahn took statements from both Matt and Lafferty, then locked Peabody up. Matt and Lafferty went home.

The trial was three weeks later and both Matt and Lafferty attended it. It was very brief. Spahn had ridden out the day after the attempted killing and had read the tracks. His testimony and that of Lafferty and Matt took less than half an hour. The jury went out and came back two hours later with a verdict of guilty. Peabody drew a sentence of six months in jail.

Standing in the tiny railroad station, Matt's mouth was suddenly grim. The law had not failed Lafferty. The one time he had tried it, he had not been disappointed.

Sourly Matt began to pace back and forth again. Memories continued to fill his thoughts. But now, his expression softened with his memories.

CHAPTER 17

Link did not change. And because he could not stand his thoughts, his own terrible sense of failure, Lafferty threw his energies into enlarging Two-Bar.

This time it was sheep. He bought thousands of them and hired Mexican and Basque sheepherders to care for them. He began construction of a textile mill, again traveling East to hire men who understood the business.

While in the East, he saw a wild West show. He returned fired with enthusiasm and determination to have his own wild West show. It would publicize Two-Bar, he said. It would advertise Two-Bar's canned meats, and textiles, and lumber and marble.

A year passed, while Lafferty gathered together Indians, trick riders, marksmen, bronc riders, and ropers.

More than ever now, Matt felt lost on Two-Bar. He knew less than half its employees, even by sight. There were times when he felt like a stranger here, a stranger who did not belong. The feeling strengthened his determination to leave. But he did not leave. Always, his leaving was a thing for the future, when Lafferty needed him no more.

Mostly Two-Bar ran itself, even when Lafferty was gone. The packing plant was a separate entity, with its own management, its own clerical force. The textile mill also was a separate entity. And a new building went up not far from the house for the clerical employees that kept an eye on the operation as a whole.

Great sacks of mail went out every week, taken to San Juan by buckboard, and great sacks of mail came back with it.

A single, thin letter came for Matt in one of those sacks, six months after Lafferty took his wild West show East.

He was up in the mountains, riding through the forest of stumps left by the timber cutters not far from one of the sawmills. He saw Julio, the Indian tracker, riding toward him, following trail.

Grinning faintly to himself, he stopped. He watched Julio ride across a stream and climb a slope toward him. He yelled and raised a hand. Julio left the trail and galloped toward him.

Julio had aged in the years that had passed since he trailed the four rustlers for Lafferty. There was gray in his black hair and new lines in his face. But his eyes remained the same, steady, calm, sometimes almost fierce with his loyalty to Lafferty and to Matt. He halted and handed the letter to Matt. Matt took it, smiling. "Somebody knew who it would take to find me, didn't they Julio?"

"Sì, señor."

Matt stared at the letter. It was addressed in Lafferty's handwriting and was postmarked Kansas City. He tore it open.

He was not a very good reader, having never gone to school. But the colonel had taught him enough so that he could read Lafferty's own simple words.

It read: "Matt: Have found Laura Peabody. If you still want her, you can find her in Westport, Missouri. Show doing good. Be home in about a month." It was signed "Lafferty."

For a moment, Matt stared blankly at the letter in his hand. Then he read it over. Julio watched him attentively.

Matt glanced up at him as Julio asked, "Trouble, señor?" He said, "No trouble, Julio. I just think maybe I'll take me a little trip."

He touched his spurs to his horse's sides and headed for the home place. Julio kept pace with him, riding silently.

Matt had never been farther from home

than Santa Fe. Now he was going to Missouri. He was going to find Laura. And he couldn't help feeling excited at the prospect. But he also felt a little scared. What if she didn't want to see him? What if she had changed?

He reached the house and got a small sack of gold coins from his room. He saddled a fresh horse and headed for San Juan.

He reached town in early evening. He found a mercantile store that was still open and bought himself a suit. He tried on several hats and finally selected a brown derby. He felt foolish with a belted gun around his middle so he left the cartridge and holster with the storekeeper and stuffed his revolver into his belt. He bought a cheap valise and put razor, soap, and towels into it, as well as a change of underwear and socks and several clean shirts. Carrying the valise, he headed for the stage depot.

The stage did not leave until ten. Matt sat in the station, feeling uncomfortable and ridiculous. His fear of seeing Laura kept growing inside of him. Several times he almost got up and left, but each time he settled back determinedly. Maybe she had changed. Maybe she wouldn't want him now. But she'd have to tell him that herself.

The stage came in at last and Matt

climbed into it. He was the only passenger.

The coach lurched and jolted away the miles. Near midnight Matt fell asleep, but it was not a deep or comfortable sleep. At intervals he would be awakened by a particularly savage lurch.

The stage wound north toward Santa Fe. It stopped once in the early morning hours for a change of horses. It stopped again at about eight, and Matt had breakfast with the driver in the way-station dining room. Afterward the coach went on.

Days and nights passed and the miles fell steadily behind. From Santa Fe, the stage road followed the old Santa Fe Trail. San Miguel. Las Vegas. Cimarron Spring. Cimarron Crossing. Pawnee Rock. Council Grove. Matt felt as though he had been in this jolting vehicle for weeks. Every bone, every muscle ached. He got so he hated to climb back into the coach after each stop.

But the jolting went on. And at last, one morning, he saw the shine of the Missouri River ahead.

Westport was no larger than Santa Fe. But it was different. The buildings were different and so were the people. There was an air of hurry here that was missing in Santa Fe.

Matt climbed down in front of the stage

depot, brushing at his clothes in a futile attempt to get the dust of the journey off, and rubbing his whiskered face. He went inside, got himself a room, and had a tub and water brought in. He bathed and shaved and brushed his suit as best he could. Then he set out to look for Laura.

At first, he just wandered the streets aimlessly. Half the day passed without results. Then he conceived the idea of inquiring after her at the stores. He figured the dressmakers' shops would be the best bet, and his guess brought results. At the third one, he was given Laura's address by a reluctant middle-aged woman who peered over her gold-rimmed glasses at Matt suspiciously.

Following directions, Matt found the house. It was a huge, three-story frame house, liberally decorated with scrollwork around the gables and eaves. There was a wrought-iron fence around the yard and a sagging porch. He twisted the bell on the door and waited impatiently.

The door was answered by an elderly woman, also wearing gold-rimmed spectacles. Matt said, "I'd like to see Miss Laura Peabody. Tell her Matt Wyatt is here."

The woman nodded sourly at him and closed the door. Matt waited nervously. At last the door flung open and Laura stood there staring unbelievingly at him.

He said, "Laura," and grinned foolishly, unable to go on.

Her voice was a whisper. "Is it really you? Oh, Matt . . ." She came out and stood for a moment no more than a foot away from him staring up at his face.

She had changed. She was older — less of a girl — more of a woman. He said. "It's me, all right."

Her hand went up fearfully to touch one of the scars her father's fists had left on his face. Her hand was soft, cool. . . . And suddenly she was in his arms, her body trembling violently. He held her close for a long, long time — until the trembling quieted. She drew away and sat down on the porch steps. Matt sat beside her. He asked, "Why? Why did you let him send you away?"

For a long time she would not look at him. Tears rolled silently down her cheeks. At last she whispered, "He said he'd kill you, Matt. He said he'd almost killed you that night and that if I saw you again, he would. I believed him, Matt. I still believe him. He will kill you."

Matt grinned at her. "It's been tried before. I'm not afraid of anything he can do. I can take care of myself and I can take care of you. I want to marry you. Here. Today.

And then I want to take you home."

Her face was white and her mouth trembled helplessly.

Matt said, "He can't hurt us, Laura. Once we're married, he won't even try."

As if to postpone her decision, she began to talk excitedly. "I saw Colonel Lafferty, Matt. I saw his show. He was here a little over a month ago."

"He wrote me that you were here."

She chattered on almost hysterically until Matt said, "Laura, stop it. I want you to marry me."

She stopped talking and stared at his face. Her eyes were enormous, filled with doubt, as plainly seeking reassurance as if she had asked for it in words. He said firmly, "Your father won't hurt me, Laura. Once we're married, he won't even try. He isn't a fool."

"Oh, I wish I could believe that, Matt."

He bent his head and kissed her lightly on the mouth. "Believe it, Laura. I do. I want you. I love you."

Her doubt lingered a while longer. Then it began to dissipate like ground fog before the morning sun. He stood up and reached for her hand. He drew her to her feet. "Go pack a bag. And hurry. We've already waited too long."

She ran into the house. He could hear her

talking, and sometimes could hear the older woman's voice. But he could not understand the words.

Laura came out. She carried a small valise. A coat was flung over her arm and she wore a flowered hat. Matt asked, "Where's the nearest church?"

She pointed. "Two blocks down and a block over."

"Let's go, then."

They walked along the tree-shaded, dusty street. Matt carried her bag in one hand and held hers with the other. It seemed like a long walk to him but at last they reached the church.

Matt waited on the sidewalk while Laura went to the door of the parsonage. She went inside and came out a few minutes later with the minister. He escorted them to the church.

As they entered it, a horseman pounded up the street and stopped at the picket gate. He got down and strode into the church. He wore a gun and the star on his shirt caught and reflected the sunlight.

"What's going on here?"

The minister said, "These two young folks want to be married, Phil."

"Married? Miss Peabody didn't say anything about marriage."

Matt glanced at Laura. "That was your aunt?"

She nodded. "She told me she'd stop me." Her face was frightened.

Matt said, "Are you going to stop us from getting married, Sheriff?"

The man shrugged. "How can I stop you? Go ahead with it. You're both old enough. I'll be one of your witnesses."

The minister got his wife and led the party into the church. Matt and Laura stood before him, holding hands. When the time came for it, the minister handed Matt a plain gold wedding band. He slipped it onto Laura's finger.

Then it was over and they were hurrying toward the stage depot. And the long journey home began.

They traveled all the rest of that day and spent their wedding night in a stage station fifteen or twenty miles west.

For them both, it was a night of awkwardness. But it was a night of beauty too. When morning came, Laura's fear of her father seemed to be gone. She seemed no longer worried about anything he might try to do.

Matt felt strong, and good, and very capable of protecting Laura from her father or from anyone else. But he did not believe her father would give up without trying. He knew Peabody better than that. The man would do something — of that he was very sure.

They would stay at Two-Bar for a while, he thought. Later, when he knew where he wanted to go, they'd go away.

He smiled at Laura and talked with her endlessly. He hid the worry he felt behind a confident smile. But the worry remained, growing as the distance grew shorter between the rattling stage and Two-Bar ranch.

And he admitted the disadvantage he would be under in the coming encounter with Peabody. He could not kill the man — not Laura's father, no matter what he did.

But Peabody could kill him — and would — the first time he got the chance.

CHAPTER 18

In Santa Fe, as they passed through on the stagecoach, the talk was of the railroad, soon to be built into Santa Fe. Matt wondered if Lafferty would succeed in having a spur run down to Two-Bar. He supposed the colonel would. Lafferty had never lagged when it came to progress. In fact, most of the progress that had come to this part of New Mexico had come because of Colonel Lafferty.

But his thoughts did not stay long with the railroad or with Lafferty. He had Laura now. And he knew her father too well to feel secure.

When they arrived at Two-Bar, he moved into the main part of the house with Laura because he knew Lafferty would have insisted on it had he been here.

The following month was a time of happiness for Matt. For the first time in his life, he felt that he belonged. He was no longer just a waif that Lafferty had picked up on the Texas plain. He was no longer Lafferty's shadow. He was an individual. He felt the urge to do things independently — for himself — for Laura — for the family they would someday have. More than ever he wanted to get out from under Lafferty's shadow, and he began to plan how he could tell the colonel that he meant to leave.

He supposed Peabody knew about the marriage by now. His sister would have written him immediately, of course. And while mail deliveries were slow, Peabody should have received her letter within a couple of weeks after their return.

So he waited, knowing Peabody would do something but having no idea what it would be. He tried to hide his worry from Laura, without success.

Laura herself became increasingly nervous. She bolted the doors carefully every night. She never left the house except when she was with Matt. She watched the empty land in the direction of town worriedly.

Matt took his own precautions. He stationed two guards out in the courtyard at night. He kept half a dozen of the men he trusted most at the home place continuously. And he never went outside without his gun strapped around his waist.

Scouting in the daytime, he found places from which the house had been watched. He would find half a dozen wheat-straw cigarette stubs on a knoll half a mile from the house. He would find a spot behind a clump of brush where someone had squatted on his heels the better part of a day. Once, he surprised one of them and watched the man pound furiously toward San Juan on his horse.

But he tired of waiting eventually. He told Laura one morning, "He's making us live scared. He's practically making prisoners of us. I'm going to bring him out into the open. Then we'll see what he's got in mind."

Laura's face lost color when he said, "I'll get you a horse. I want you to ride away, like you were just going for a ride. I'll keep an eye on you, and I won't let anything happen. All right?"

She nodded, her eyes fixed on his face. He put his arms around her gently. She had confidence in him. He had seen that in her face. But she was still afraid — afraid of her father and of what he might do.

He got her a horse and brought it to the house. He watched her ride away, and he watched the land around the house until she had disappeared from sight.

He saw the watcher come from concealment, mount his horse, and ride toward town. He mounted his own horse and went after Laura to bring her back.

Every day after that, Laura went for a

ride. And every day, just before dawn, half a dozen men rode out to conceal themselves along her route.

On the sixth day, Laura went for her ride as usual. Matt, hidden in a dry wash with his horse a couple of miles from the house, watched patiently as she approached his hiding place.

He saw them appear from behind a rise while she was still a mile away from him. But he stayed where he was and watched her turn toward him and urge her horse into a gallop. She came on, face white, hair whipping out behind her, and, following the instructions he had given her earlier, put her horse down into the wash and dismounted at his side.

Now, from behind her pursuers, Matt's six men appeared. Peabody and his men glanced around at them, then urged their horses to an even greater speed.

A mile separated Peabody and his men from Matt's pursuing six. He grinned to himself humorlessly. They thought they had time to catch Laura and get away. But they didn't know Matt was here with her.

While they were still a couple of hundred yards away, Matt levered a cartridge into his rifle. He sighted carefully on the chest of Peabody's horse. At a range of a hundred and fifty yards, he squeezed the trigger carefully.

The rifle kicked against his shoulder. He saw Peabody's horse go down.

Peabody went over the horse's head, rolled, then got to his feet. He stared furiously toward Matt. Matt yelled, "Shuck your guns, the whole damn bunch of you!"

One man took a shot at him. Matt ducked, then poked his head up and squeezed off a second shot. The man's horse reared and fell over backward. The man, caught beneath him, screamed with pain.

Laura gasped with fright. Matt said sharply, "Stay down!"

Peabody's men dropped their guns and raised their hands but Peabody did not. Matt's six men came up behind them, guns drawn. Peabody glared for several moments more, then reluctantly dropped his gun. Matt climbed out of the wash.

He walked toward the group. He said, "You're trespassing, Peabody." He had never seen, in the face of any man, more pure, undiluted hatred than he now saw in Peabody's face. The man's eyes blazed. His face was almost gray. He was trembling with fury and seemed, for the moment, unable even to speak.

When he could speak, he said hoarsely, "I want my daughter! I want her now! You tricked her into marrying you. You dirty . . ."

Matt turned his head. "Laura."

She climbed out of the wash and approached. She took a place at his side.

He glanced down at her face. It was white and her eyes were terrified. She was trembling violently. But her gaze did not falter. She looked squarely at her father. "I'm Matt's wife, Father. I'm his wife because I want to be. I intend to stay with him."

The veins on Peabody's forehead bulged. Involuntarily, Matt raised his gun, thumb on the hammer. He thought for a moment that Peabody would attack him in spite of it.

But Peabody did not. His effort at self-control was tremendous. In the end he won, though the malevolence in his eyes did not diminish. Even as he turned away, Matt had the sudden certainty that, sooner or later, he would have to kill Peabody or Peabody would kill him.

Peabody stared at his dead horse. Without a word, he walked to one of his men and mounted awkwardly behind him. The man who had been pinned by the horse was free now. He hobbled painfully to another of the men and, with great difficulty, was hoisted up behind the saddle. The group turned silently away.

Matt released a long, slow sigh. He put an arm around Laura and found that she was trembling uncontrollably. He got her horse and helped her mount. He rode back with her toward home.

She glanced at him and spoke in a whisper, "What will he do now?"

Matt frowned. "He won't do this again, at least."

He could feel his own anger rising. It wasn't right for them to have to live this way, terrified all the time of what Peabody might do. Nor could he guess what the man would do next. It might be anything. He might try to ambush Matt, knowing Matt's death to be the only thing that would bring his daughter back.

He knew a bleak feeling of hopelessness, because no matter what happened, he couldn't win. Peabody would force the issue eventually. And if he wasn't killed himself, he would kill Peabody. Either way, his life with Laura would be at an end.

Months passed uneventfully after that. Lafferty returned with his wild West show after a highly successful tour.

The rails crawled westward. In 1880, they

214

reached Santa Fe, and crawled on south. The following spring the first locomotive reached San Juan and that summer a spur line ran across Two-Bar to the cannery.

Laura was still afraid to go to San Juan alone, and Matt was afraid to let her go. Peabody had done nothing since the day he'd tried to kidnap her, but Matt knew Peabody hadn't quit. Sooner or later, his hatred of Two-Bar would get the best of him.

Peabody's action, when it came, was unexpected and sudden. And he struck not at Matt but at Link Lafferty.

Laura was six months pregnant and showed it, but she refused to stay in the house and she wanted her father to know. So one day Matt took her in to San Juan.

Taking her to Peabody's house was against his better judgment. But he drove Laura in a buggy and halted it in front of Peabody's house. He walked to the door with Laura and twisted the bell.

They waited uneasily. He doubted if fear was good for Laura but he also knew she had do to this for her own peace of mind.

Peabody himself answered the door. He glared at Matt and at Laura. She said softly, "Father, I've got to talk to you."

"Talk? I've nothing to say to you."

"I'm going to have a child. I thought you would want to know."

Peabody's face lost color, but his eyes lost none of their coldness. He said savagely, "A Two-Bar brat! Get out of here! I don't want to see you again."

Matt took Laura's arm but she pulled away. She said, "Father, please . . ."

He glared at her a moment more. Then he deliberately stepped back and slammed the door.

Laura was weeping softly as they walked to the buggy and climbed inside. Matt picked up the reins and drove away. They reached Two-Bar late that night. Laura cried softly beside Matt until she finally fell asleep.

Matt lay awake long after that, sometimes frowning, sometimes cursing beneath his breath. Peabody was consumed by hatred and would never give it up. Nor was there anything he could do to make the fact easier for Laura to accept. She was no longer Peabody's daughter. She was a part of Two-Bar now, and hated as the rest of Two-Bar was.

But Matt underestimated Peabody's anguish over learning of his daughter's pregnancy. That same night, Peabody struck out blindly at Two-Bar. Because Link happened to be handiest, he struck out at him.

A teamster, returning to Two-Bar with an empty wagon, brought Link home. He had been treated by a doctor in San Juan and was swathed with bandages. His left arm was broken in two places. He had been beaten until he was scarcely recognizable.

Fortunately, Lafferty had gone East again or he would have killed Peabody himself. As it was, Matt sent a man into San Juan to swear out a warrant for Peabody's arrest. And Link lay for two whole weeks in bed before he could get up.

Link would say little to Matt about the attack except to tell him that Peabody was the one. And since Link had never been very communicative, Matt gave it little thought. Peabody went to trial and was fined a hundred dollars and costs.

But that was not the end of it. Not for Link, at least. As soon as he could ride, he got a horse and set out for town.

Matt might have tried to stop him if he'd seen him go. But Link had been gone two hours before Matt even knew he had left. He saddled a horse immediately and headed for San Juan himself.

Several times during the long ride to town, he was struck by a parallel. Years before he had nearly killed a horse trying to get into town in time to stop Lafferty from hanging the rustlers. It was possible, of course, that Link had nothing violent in mind at all. Maybe he just wanted a woman, or wanted to get drunk. But Matt didn't believe it. He knew Link too well. He knew the smoldering hatred, the sleeping violence in Link.

Reaching town, he rode straight to Spahn's office. It occupied the front part of the adobe jail, and there was a crowd in front of it.

Spahn opened the door as he dismounted. Matt asked, "Seen Link, Sheriff?"

Spahn nodded. "He's here. Come in."

Matt went in. Spahn closed the door. Matt said, "I'll bail him out. What's he done this time?"

Spahn glanced at him strangely. He said, "I'm holding him without bail on a murder charge. You can see him if you want."

Matt held his breath. At last he asked, "Peabody?"

Spahn nodded. "Shot down unarmed." His eyes hardened. "I never had much use for Peabody. But this . . . Jesus, Link emptied his gun into him and then beat him over the head with it. He had to be dragged off."

Matt said, "Let me see him."

Spahn led him toward the rear of the jail.

He opened a door and let Matt precede him.

Link was sitting on a wooden bench, his head hanging. His broken arm was still in a sling, but the sling was stained with blood and dirt. Matt said, "Link."

Link looked up. He stared at Matt with dislike apparent in his sullen eyes.

Matt said, "I'll telegraph your father."

Link shrugged disinterestedly.

Matt asked gently, "Anything you want?"

Link shook his head. He stared at the floor between his feet.

Matt turned and went back out front. He told himself that Link's own nature had gotten him into this. He told himself it had been inevitable from the first. And perhaps it had.

But he couldn't help feeling responsible. Peabody had taken out his hatred of Lafferty and of Matt on Link by beating him. Link had been fighting both Matt's and Lafferty's battles when he killed the man. Mistakenly and wrongly, certainly. But that didn't lessen Matt's feeling of responsibility. He mounted and rode immediately to the telegraph office in the railroad depot. He sent a half dozen telegrams to half a dozen different places he thought Lafferty might be. Then he mounted and turned toward home.

He had to tell Laura and he dreaded it. But even more than that he dreaded Lafferty's return.

CHAPTER 19

The storm was gone, and so were the clouds. The land lay steaming beneath the hot rays of the afternoon sun. Matt went outside onto the station platform and stared down the track in the direction from which the train would come. The air was hot and humid now and he could feel sweat springing from his pores.

Colonel Lafferty came out and began to pace back and forth — up and down the soggy station platform. Matt was reminded again of a painting he had once seen of Napoleon. All Lafferty needed was the greatcoat and three-cornered hat.

Matt had always feared this ultimate violence and had known it would surely come. Yet now that it had come, he resisted it, disputing that it was the end of everything.

He could leave now, of course. He could repudiate all that the colonel had done for him, and run out just when Lafferty needed him the most. Laura would take him back if he did. He might live to see his son born, might see him grow to maturity.

His jaw hardened against the sudden ache

in his heart. He turned his head and stared at Lafferty. Living built obligations, he thought, that an honest man could not deny. His obligation to Lafferty was one. If he repudiated Lafferty he repudiated everything, his own honesty, his own loyalty. He would be no man afterward. He would be something shameful, living in a man's body, making a pretense of honor before the world.

He walked back into the station and stared up at the clock hanging on the wall. Only twenty minutes more. In twenty minutes the train would come puffing in and the gunmen Saxon had hired would be piling off. Then it would be too late for anything — anything but death.

It had taken Lafferty three days to get home after Matt telegraphed him. He came in a special train — an engine tender, and a single car. He came through on a cleared track. And because he had telegraphed ahead, Matt was waiting when the train pulled in.

Lafferty got off and strode immediately to Matt. The first thing he asked was, "Did he do it, Matt? Did he kill Peabody?"

Matt nodded. "Spahn's got a dozen eyewitnesses."

"And it was like you said — he emptied

his gun and then beat Peabody with it?"

Matt nodded wordlessly.

Lafferty turned his head and yelled at the engineer, "Turn that thing around and keep steam up. I'll be going to Santa Fe."

The train puffed away. Matt asked, "What are you going to do?"

Suddenly the decisiveness, the strength was gone from Lafferty. He stared at Matt with bleak despair. "I don't know, Matt. I just don't know."

Matt said, "If you're thinking of breaking him out, give it up. Spahn's taking no chances with him. He's called in troops from Fort Union. They got here yesterday. They've got a twenty-four-hour guard around the jail."

Lafferty glanced up. "I wasn't thinking of breaking him out."

He strode stiffly away, heading for the jail. Matt followed him. At the jail, Spahn relieved them of their guns before he would let them go inside.

Link was sitting on the same bench in the same cell. He glanced up at his father with the same smoldering, sullen look he had given Matt several days before. He asked, "Come to see me hang?"

"You're not going to hang."

"The hell I'm not. Even you can't change that."

"I'll change it. You sit tight. And don't worry."

Link gave him a long, steady look. Matt got the impression that Link was less worried than relieved. His destiny had at last been snatched out of his own hands. He was like a train on a track now, heading for a definite, predetermined end.

Lafferty shook his head wonderingly. He said, "Link, don't you care?"

Something like anger came to Link's eyes, eyes that had always been older than his years. He said, "No. I don't care. I don't give a damn. Now go away and let me be."

Lafferty went out and Matt followed him. Lafferty strode to the station, boarded his train, and went to Santa Fe. He returned two days later, half an hour before Link's trial. He told Matt as the two sat in the hushed courtroom, "I talked to the governor. I think I can get Link's sentence commuted after the trial."

The judge called the court to order. Link sat at a table with the attorney, Leonard Lewis. He was shackled and there were soldiers at the door and outside in the hall. All the spectators had been disarmed.

The prosecuting attorney presented his case. It was dispassionate and thorough. He called the witnesses to the killing, one by one. Each gave substantially the same testimony. Link had emptied his gun into Peabody. When it was empty he had beaten Peabody's head to a bloody pulp, stopping only when he had been forcibly dragged away.

Matt stared at the jury, at each juryman's face in turn. Their faces were hard, uncompromising.

The defense attorney, Lewis, presented his case. Matt tried to convince himself that it was strong enough to give Link a chance. Lewis brought out how Peabody and his men had beaten Link, savagely, mercilessly, and without reason. He brought out the deathless hatred Peabody had felt toward Lafferty and Matt and Two-Bar ranch. He brought out the fact that Link had been the helpless victim of this hatred.

Both sides summarized and the judge gave his instructions to the jury. They retired.

They were out ten minutes. Few of the spectators had even left the courtroom. They filed back in and the judge asked, "Have you reached a verdict?"

"We have, your honor!"

"What is your verdict?"

"We find the defendant guilty as charged."

Matt felt Lafferty stiffen beside him. He glanced aside at Lafferty's face. It was terrible. The eyes blazed with fury. His mouth was compressed, his lips almost blue.

The judge said, "The defendant will rise and face the jury."

Lewis nudged Link, who seemed dazed. Link stood up. The judge said, "You have been found guilty of murder in the first degree. Have you anything to say before I pronounce sentence?"

Link shook his head sullenly.

The judge glanced across at Lafferty. Turning back to Link, he said, "I sentence you to be hanged by the neck until you are dead. Sentence will be carried out at dawn on the morning of June 16th." He struck the bench three times with his gavel. "Court is dismissed."

The silence that hung over the room suddenly exploded into noise. Voices shouted. Matt heard one, rising above the others, "That'll teach the son-of-a-bitch, by God! That'll fix Lafferty!"

Half a dozen men laughed.

Beside him, Lafferty was trembling, as though he had a chill. Matt touched his arm. "Come on, Colonel. Let's get out of here."

He pushed through the crowd and for

once the colonel was content to follow him. Twice, Matt flung a man bodily out of his way. The laughter went out of the crowd long before they reached the door and the sound they made became angry and menacing. The two soldiers at the door pushed toward Matt and cleared the remaining distance to the door.

They reached the hall and hurried along it to the outside door. They stepped out into the sunlight.

Lafferty seemed to have aged twenty years. He seemed suddenly like a frail old man. His face sagged; his eyes were spiritless. His mouth was slack and trembling. Matt said, "Colonel! Pull yourself together. It ain't the end of the world."

"It's my fault he's in there. They didn't try him, they tried me. And they convicted me. But it's him they'll hang."

"Maybe not. You said the governor might commute . . ."

A spark came back to Lafferty. He said, "Yes. I did say that, didn't I?"

He turned and strode toward the railroad depot. He got aboard his private train, and this time, Matt went along.

They must have broken all records on that run to Santa Fe. When they arrived, it was night. Lafferty and Matt left the train and took a carriage to the governor's mansion. They woke him and got him out of bed.

Matt knew, the instant he saw the governor, that it was no use. The governor had a sheaf of telegrams in his hand. He said, "Colonel, there's over a hundred of these here. They all came in today. Not one of 'em wants your son released. Every single one of them wants the sentence carried out — without interference from me."

"I could remind you of a few things, Governor."

The governor nodded reluctantly. "You could, Colonel. And they'd all be true. But I can't commute that sentence. I can't and I won't."

Lafferty exploded. He argued and pleaded. He threatened and promised and tried to bribe. None of it did any good. The governor remained adamant. And at last Lafferty gave up with the dark threat, "There are other ways, Governor. There are other ways."

"I hope you won't use them, Colonel Lafferty."

Lafferty said, "My son is not going to hang, Governor. No matter what I have to do."

All the way back to Two-Bar, Lafferty sat in brooding silence in the single railroad coach. And for the first time, Matt felt sorry for him. He seemed utterly defeated, beaten. There was nothing but bleak despair in the sagging lines of his face.

Maybe, Matt thought, defeat would be good for Colonel Lafferty. Never before had he been defeated. It might make him less arrogant.

But Matt doubted it. None of his personal failures had lessened his arrogance. If Link was executed, Lafferty would only become more bitter. And in the end he would destroy himself.

He said, "You've still got almost a month, Colonel. A lot can happen in a month. Money will open a lot of doors."

Lafferty nodded heavily. His head lifted and he scowled. At least, thought Matt, he was beginning to think and plan again. And if anyone could find a way of saving Link, Colonel Lafferty could.

CHAPTER 20

Matt went to Laura immediately when they reached Two-Bar. She smiled a wan welcome at him and he kissed her worriedly.

She seemed weaker than she ever had before. He said, "The governor refused to commute the sentence or interfere in any way. He showed us more than a hundred telegrams."

Laura did not look at him. "What will Colonel Lafferty do now?"

Matt shrugged. "What can he do? He can't fight the United States Government. Spahn has soldiers from Fort Union guarding the jail. There's a whole troop of cavalry in San Juan. Lafferty can't get Link's sentence changed and he can't get him out of jail."

He studied her, deep concern in his eyes. "How do you feel?"

"I'm all right." She smiled. "In another couple of months it will be over. We'll have a son, Matt. A son just like you."

"How do you know it's going to be a son?"

"Because that's what I want." Her smile

faded slowly and the worry returned to her eyes. "I wish I didn't feel so responsible for what has happened. If we hadn't gone to Father and told him about the baby . . . he wouldn't have beaten Link. And Link wouldn't have killed him."

"It might have happened anyway. Your father wasn't exactly predictable."

He talked with her a while longer. She seemed to tire quickly. At last he got up. "You get some rest. I'm worried about you."

"I'm all right, Matt. But I think I will lie down."

Matt went outside. Lafferty yelled at him, and Matt crossed the courtyard to him. Lafferty was a changed man. No longer did defeat show in his face and eyes. He was his old, firm, decisive self. He said, "Matt, I want you to take a trip. Go to Dodge City. Take that train we used to go to Santa Fe. I want some men — fifty — sixty if you can get that many. Gunfighters. Buffalo hunters. Anybody that will do what he's told if he's paid enough. Promise 'em a thousand dollars apiece."

"What are you going to do with them?"

"What do you think, Matt? I'm going to get Link out of jail."

"There's a troop of cavalry in San Juan."

"This is a local matter, Matt. The cavalry won't interfere."

"The hell they won't! You know what Spahn had to do to get 'em in the first place? He had to tell the Army the law had broken down."

"They won't interfere." Lafferty's voice was stubborn now.

Matt stared. Lafferty had never refused to face reality before, and the cavalry was a reality. They were in San Juan to preserve order, at the request of local authorities. They wouldn't be bluffed by Lafferty and they wouldn't stay out of it.

Lafferty glanced at him. "What the hell are you waiting for? You haven't got a bit more time than you're going to need. Get moving."

Matt shook his head. "I'm not going to Dodge, Colonel. If you want men like that, send someone else."

Lafferty's voice was unbelieving. "You've never . . ."

"I've never refused to do anything you asked me to, have I? Well, maybe it's time I did. Peabody was wrong when he beat up Link. Link was wrong when he killed him because of it. Now you're wrong. If you take on Spahn and the town and the U.S. Cavalry, thirty or forty men are going to be killed. It'll be the end of you, and me, and Two-Bar, and a hell of a lot of other things."

"I can send Saxon if you won't go."

"Send him then. Because I can't go. Link killed Laura's father. She wouldn't have wanted me to avenge him, but neither will she want me to take a hand in getting his killer off. I'm over a barrel, Colonel. I've got my tail in a crack."

Lafferty nodded. "I didn't think of that. I guess you have got your tail in a crack. All right. I'll send Les."

He stalked away. Matt watched him go, frowning worriedly. It was obvious that the colonel was desperate. It was also obvious that he was casting caution to the winds. He'd do anything he had to do to keep Link from being hanged.

An unbearable guilt kept pushing him. He felt that he'd failed Link from the time Link was old enough to walk. He knew that if he let Link die it would torment him all the rest of his life. He would have lost the last connection he had with Lily. He would have lost the last thing that made life bearable.

Matt stared around, at the house, at the buildings, at the humming activity. Lafferty had succeeded in everything he tried to do with respect to the ranch. He had failed at everything connected with his personal life.

It was a bitter irony, but it was true. Matt promised himself suddenly that he wouldn't make the same mistake.

An hour later, the train pulled away, with Les Saxon aboard. He had twenty-five thousand dollars of the colonel's money and he had orders to be back before June 15. With at least fifty men.

That night, Matt told Laura what Lafferty had done. She looked at him steadily as he talked. "And what will you do, Matt?"

"Do? What do you mean?"

She smiled. "I know your loyalty for him. I think I have always been afraid that some day you would have to make a choice."

"What kind of choice?" Matt felt a sinking sensation in his stomach, a feeling that was almost nausea, a feeling that was pure, cold fear. He knew what Laura meant. That he must choose, now, between her and his son and Colonel Lafferty. He must choose, as well, between what was right and his stubborn loyalty.

Laura said softly, "I love you, Matt. I love you more than life. Take me away — now, while there's still time."

Matt stared at the floor between his feet. He said, "Laura, you've got to understand how it is between Lafferty and me. He found me down in Texas after the Indians killed my folks. If it hadn't been for him, I'd be dead. He brought me up here to New Mexico and we started from scratch. I've watched Two-Bar grow from nothing. I had a big hand in it myself. It's part of me and so is Lafferty. A man doesn't turn his back on . . ."

Her voice was firm, but it was also scared. "You've got to turn your back, Matt. He'll squeeze the last drop of blood from you. He'll get you killed. You have a new obligation now. To me and to our son."

He raised his glance to her face. His voice was tortured. "I can't! I can't leave him when he needs me more than he ever has before."

"He'll always need you, Matt. Don't you see that? He'll need you more with every day that passes. Do you know why? Because he's getting weaker and you're getting stronger as he does."

Matt had never thought of it that way before. But he supposed she was right. And yet, how could he walk out on Lafferty when the colonel was about to lose his last close tie? He said, "We'll go, Laura, but I can't go before the 16th of June. I can't!"

"Then we'll never go. Because you'll be dead."

There was silence between them for a

long, long time. At last Laura said, "I had hoped I would never have to say this to you, Matt." Her voice was so low he could scarcely hear. He glanced up and saw tears spilling from her eyes, running across her flawless cheeks.

"Say what?" His voice was steady but there was something cold in his chest.

"That if you help Lafferty break my father's killer out of jail . . . if you take part in an attack on the town of San Juan . . . I won't be here when you get back . . . if you do get back."

He stared at her unbelievingly. "You'd leave me? Do you really mean that?"

She met his glance steadily. "I mean it, Matt."

Anger touched him briefly and went away. He got up and began to pace restlessly back and forth. He could feel resentment growing in him — resentment toward Lafferty — toward Laura too. A man shouldn't be crowded into a position like this — forced to choose between the two he loved most in all the world.

He went outside and strode furiously across the courtyard. He got himself a horse, saddled, and rode away from the humming complex of buildings at Two-Bar headquarters.

He'd always been able to think best on a horse. He'd always had a clearer mind out in the long, empty miles of Two-Bar ranch.

He rode all the rest of that day, and slept that night in one of the tiny adobe line shacks at the western edge of the ranch. He rode all the next day too, his forehead lined with worry and uncertainty.

Half a dozen times he made up his mind to take Laura and leave. Half a dozen times he changed it again and decided he would have to stay with Lafferty to the bitter end. When he returned to the house at the end of the second day, he still did not know what he was going to do.

He told himself Laura wouldn't really leave, but he didn't believe it. Nor would it actually matter much, because he wouldn't be coming back. Neither he nor Lafferty would come back.

There was strain between Laura and himself. But between Lafferty and himself there was more closeness than there had ever been before, and Matt understood its cause. Lafferty was afraid, perhaps for the first time in his life. Not afraid of death, but of the certainty of failure that was facing him.

Lafferty knew his life was almost done. He knew he couldn't win but he also knew he couldn't quit.

He was just like Link had been in that respect, Matt thought sadly. He was like a train on a track, roaring along toward a predetermined end, toward a crash at the end of track. He couldn't stop and he couldn't turn aside.

And Matt knew, though he had not yet admitted it even to himself, that there was only one decision he could make. He had shared the good years with Lafferty. He could not now shirk at the bitter end.

CHAPTER 21

Matt Wyatt's face was bleak as he stared along the track. In the distance, now, he could see a thin plume of black smoke. He turned and called, "It's comin', Colonel."

Lafferty came out onto the station platform and followed Matt's glance along the track. He nodded curtly. He turned his head and looked at Matt. He said, "Matt, I . . ."

He couldn't go on. He cleared his throat and finally said, "We've come a long way together, Matt. If this don't come off . . . Well, I made a will a couple of days ago. If Link and I don't come through and you do . . ." Again he stopped, choked with emotion and unable to go on.

Matt had never felt more admiration for the little colonel than he did right now. Lafferty was convinced he was going to die. Furthermore, he was convinced he could not save Link. A lesser man would have given up. But not Lafferty. He didn't know what it was to quit.

The Mexican woman came out onto the station platform, followed by her children. They stood in a group, glancing first in the direction from which the train was coming and then, uneasily, at Matt and Lafferty. Even the children seemed to sense what was in the air.

The smoke plume grew slowly and at last the tall stack of the engine became visible. The train whistled, the plume of white steam from the whistle visible a long time before the sound reached their ears.

There was no nervousness now in Matt. He watched the train grow in size as it approached.

A hundred yards from the station, the engineer cut his speed and applied the brakes. The train ground noisily to a halt.

Les Saxon was the first out of the coach. He strode to the colonel and stuck out his hand. Lafferty took it. Saxon said, "I got some good ones, Colonel Lafferty. They'll put up a fight for you."

Lafferty nodded and Saxon glanced at Matt. "I wasn't sure you'd be here, Matt."

Matt grinned wryly at him. "Neither was I." He turned his head and watched Saxon's gunmen pile off the train.

They were about what he had expected. Buffalo hunters. A few trail hands. A nondescript little man no one would even notice in a crowd unless they noticed the way his gun was hung and the coldness of his eyes. A big man, carefully dressed in a suit, with a flowing mustache and hair that reached his shoulders. Several that were plainly ex-Army men. One in a Confederate cap so old it couldn't help but remind Matt that the war had been over fifteen years. And a dozen border-town cutthroats that Matt wouldn't have turned his back on in broad daylight. Several of the fifty Matt recognized from photographs.

Lafferty roared at them to form on the platform. They did so slowly, making a ragged line.

Lafferty paced up and down in front of them. He roared, "You've each been paid five hundred dollars. There will be another five hundred for each of you tonight."

He waited a moment, then went on, "You all understand that for a thousand dollars, there is risk involved. We're going to break the jail in San Juan. They'll be expecting us. There will be a fight. If you all give a good account of yourselves, we will succeed. If we fail, you will get no more money because I won't be around to pay it to you."

A man's hoarse voice shouted, "Somebody said somethin' about cavalry. What about that, Colonel Lafferty?"

"There's a troop of cavalry in San Juan. About thirty men, I think. But it's not a cavalry affair and I doubt if they'll interfere. If they do, we fight them. Nobody promised you this would be a cinch."

He paced back and forth, staring first at one, then at another. "Any more questions?"

The train chugged out of the station. Lafferty roared above its noise, "All right, then, this is the layout of the town!" He began to sketch San Juan on the station wall with a thick pencil, talking as he drew, explaining which way they would enter the town, where the jail was, where they would be most likely to encounter resistance. It would be a frontal attack, with the entire force kept together. He wanted the town and the cavalry to know exactly how many men he had. He figured there would be less likelihood of resistance if they knew.

When he had finished outlining his plan, he again asked for questions. A couple of men asked questions and Lafferty answered them. At last he bawled, "All right, then. Get saddled. Horses and saddles are over there at the corral!"

They trooped toward the corral across the muddy ground. Lafferty and Matt followed them. Their two horses were already saddled and were tied to the corral. Matt swung to the soggy saddle and waited for the men.

They roped out horses, one by one, and saddled them. Those who finished first mounted and waited silently for the others to finish. Matt stared almost longingly in the direction of the buildings at Two-Bar ranch. He wondered if Laura had already left and where she would go. Then he turned his head and stared in the direction they would be going soon. San Juan was only about five miles from here, and this was the very edge of Two-Bar ranch.

The last straggles were saddling now. They mounted and joined the group.

Lafferty led out, with Les Saxon on one side of him, with Matt on the other side. He lifted his horse to a trot. The ground, still muddy from the rain, was slick in places and the horses sometimes floundered helplessly in it.

They left the railroad station behind. Matt glanced back once more in the direction of Two-Bar. He saw a buggy coming, hardly more than a speck in the distance.

He said quickly, "I'll catch up with you, Colonel. I think that's Laura."

Lafferty nodded without speaking. Matt turned his horse and touched his sides with the spurs. The animal broke into a lope.

At this gait, great gobs of mud were flung behind by the horse's hoofs. Matt headed past the station and pounded toward the oncoming buggy.

He knew it was Laura before he had gone half the distance separating them. He reached her a few moments later and drew his horse to a halt.

She had been driving through the rain, but it must have been blowing from behind because she was only damp. She pushed a wisp of hair back from her forehead, her eyes enormous as they rested on Matt's face. She said, "Matt, I . . . I guess I just had to try again."

He dismounted and walked to the side of the buggy. But he didn't touch her. He just stood there looking up, watching the tears that formed in her eyes, spilled over, and ran across her cheeks. He said, "You shouldn't have driven here — this far. It isn't good for you."

"You haven't changed, have you, Matt?"

He shook his head reluctantly. He said, "For twenty-five years I've been part of everything he did. I can't quit now; I can't run out on him now when things are tough." He frowned, groping for words, words that would tell her exactly how he felt. At last he said, "He's got fifty men with him, but unless I'm with him he's alone. Can you understand that, Laura?"

She nodded. She did not remind him that she was also alone without him, that their child, soon to be born, would be alone as well. Her face lost all its life and became suddenly a face without hope. He said numbly, "I've got to go, Laura, if I'm going to catch up with them."

He reached up and took her shoulders in his hands. He stared into her face for a long, long time. Then, gently, he touched her pale lips with his own.

A single sob shook her. He turned away and started to mount. Laura said softly, "Matt."

He turned his head.

"I'm not leaving you, Matt. I'll be there at the railroad station when you come back." She raised a hand and brushed away the tears. She made a small, brave smile.

Matt's throat closed. His chest felt as though it had a weight on it. He felt tears burn his own eyes and said hoarsely, "Thank you, Laura."

He wheeled his horse and sank the spurs. He glanced back once as he went past the railroad station and saw her buggy coming on. He turned his face toward San Juan and raked his horse again with the spurs. Floundering in the mud, the horse pounded on.

This reminded Matt suddenly of the time,

so many years before, when he had ridden to San Juan to try and stop the hanging of the rustlers. He hadn't felt much hope then, and he felt none now. But this time he would catch up with Lafferty. This time he would be there when the trouble began.

The miles dropped away behind. He sighted Lafferty's men and the town at almost the same time. Lafferty was still a mile short of the town's outskirts, and Matt was only a half a mile behind.

He urged his horse to even greater speed, and caught up with the stragglers while they were still more than half a mile from town. He pounded to the head of the column and slowed at Lafferty's side. The colonel looked at him. "Laura?"

Matt nodded.

"She wanted you to go back." It was a statement, not a question.

Matt nodded again.

Lafferty's jaw hardened. He kept his eyes straight ahead and his voice was strained as he said, "Go back, Matt. Go on back — now."

Matt didn't reply. It was plain to him how hard those words had come to the colonel's lips.

For several moments they rode in silence. Then, still without looking at him, Colonel

Lafferty roared, "God damn you, Matt! Did you hear me!"

"I heard you, Colonel. But I'm not going back."

Lafferty looked at him. His face was twisted, reddened with anger. But there were tears in his eyes. Matt said hoarsely, "Let's get this over with."

Lafferty nodded. Still short of the town's outskirts, he halted his horse and turned to face the men. "You remember the map I drew on the station wall for you. Keep your guns ready. I doubt if there'll be any trouble until we reach the plaza, but they won't let us get past that."

The men were silent, grim. Lafferty turned to Saxon. "Les, you bring up the rear. Keep 'em closed up. When we get to the plaza, we'll need all of 'em." He didn't exactly say it, but Matt and Les both knew what he really meant. He meant, "Don't let any of 'em drop back. Don't let any of 'em quit." Saxon also knew the rest of what he meant. "If any of 'em try to quit, gun them down."

Lafferty and Matt rode on, with the men closed up now behind. Saxon dropped back to the rear, his gun ready in his hand. They entered the narrow, alley-like streets and headed into the heart of town, toward the plaza, where they knew the fight awaited them.

At each cross street, Matt glanced to right and left, in case anyone had ideas about ambushing them. The streets were all deserted, as though this part of town had been evacuated.

Lafferty seemed to be in the grip of some powerful emotion. He kept his eyes straight ahead. His face was pale and his jaws were clenched. His hand, holding the reins, trembled visibly.

A block before they reached the plaza, he spoke without turning his head. "A man's a fool, Matt. A man's a blind, stupid fool."

Matt waited. He didn't speak because there was nothing for him to say.

Lafferty went on, speaking as though with difficulty. "A man wants a son, a part of himself to go on after he is dead. But . . ." he paused, swallowed a couple of times, then finished hoarsely, "you're more a part of me than Link ever was. The blood tie doesn't mean a goddam thing. Link's Lily's son. And I guess you're mine."

Briefly he turned his head now and looked at Matt. There was pain in his eyes, but there was something else as well. Pride. Perhaps a measure of contentment because in this last hour before he died he knew he had not failed utterly.

Matt nodded, his own throat tight. He was suddenly glad that he had come. He was glad that, because he had come, the colonel had found this small measure of peace.

Lafferty's hand abruptly stopped trembling as it held the reins. The pain as abruptly left his eyes. His mouth made a sudden, prideful grin. "We built us something, didn't we, young Matt? We really built us something when we built Two-Bar."

"You built it, Colonel Lafferty."

Lafferty shook his head. "I couldn't have built it without you, Matt. I couldn't have done a thing. Funny, isn't it? All this time I thought it was for Lily or Link. But it wasn't. It was for you and me."

Matt stared down at his saddle horn. He knew if he tried to speak, he was going to come apart. Suddenly, then, their horses left the last narrow street and came out into the open plaza.

And as suddenly, all sentiment was gone from Lafferty. His voice was sharp, a cavalry commander's voice. "Go left, Matt, and let 'em spread out between us. Let's let these bastards see how many men we got."

CHAPTER 22

Matt edged to the left immediately. Lafferty reined his prancing horse to the right. Between them, the men came out of the narrow street and spread out in a line.

They were a villainous looking lot, Matt thought as he stared along the line. But they'd turn in a good account of themselves down to the last man. Saxon would have screened them before hiring them. Matt was willing to bet not a one of them would break and run.

He glanced across the grassy plaza. Here was where Lafferty had hanged the three rustlers years ago. Here was where it had started and here was where it was going to end.

A troop of cavalry, numbering perhaps thirty men, were drawn up in formation on the far side of the plaza. On both sides of the cavalry were ragged companies of civilians, townsmen, and these numbered almost a hundred men.

Without the cavalry, it would have been easy for Lafferty. The townsmen, the hastily formed militia, would break under heavy attack. But not the cavalry. And with the cavalry to give them courage, to lead them, the militia constituted a serious threat. Besides, they were afoot. In the streets and alleyways of the town they'd be much more effective than mounted men.

Matt pulled his glance from the opposition and looked at Lafferty. Lafferty's eyes were glowing with excitement. His mouth was a thin line. His skin was flushed.

Appalled, Matt stared at him. Lafferty had led this same blue-coated cavalry during the war. It was shocking that he could fight against it now, that he who had fought to preserve the Union should now fight a treasonous rebellion to tear it down.

And Matt saw something else as he stared at Lafferty. He saw the quiet desperation of certain defeat. The colonel knew that what he was about to do was suicidal. He knew there was no chance of winning. But the old pride was driving him, the old sensitiveness about his size.

Suddenly Matt was furious. Furious at the thought of giving everything, Laura, his future, perhaps even his life for a doomed cause. He bawled, "Colonel!"

Lafferty turned his head. An expression of surprise touched his face when he saw the anger in Matt. Matt reined his horse aside and rode to where Lafferty sat his own prancing mount. Putting himself between Lafferty and the nearest man he said, "You *know* you're going to lose!"

Lafferty neither confirmed nor denied the accusation. Matt asked furiously, "Good God, don't you care? Aren't you even going to try to win?"

Lafferty scowled but he did not reply. Matt raged, "What kind of cavalry commander are you anyway? Didn't you learn anything in the war? If you send every man you've got in a frontal attack against superior odds, you're bound to lose!"

Lafferty said harshly, "Get back in position!"

"I will like hell! I'm going to take some men and circle around behind that bunch. Are you going to give me the men or do I have to take them anyway?"

From the other side of the plaza a voice suddenly roared, "Wait! Damn it, wait a minute!" The cavalry commander, a lieutenant, left the ranks of his troops and rode to one side to join a couple of other men. He dismounted and all three advanced slowly across the plaza.

Matt recognized the territorial governor. Spahn strode on one side of him, the lieutenant on the other.

This, he realized, was his chance — to take some of the men and get away from the plaza, to circle and come up on the other side. He glanced at Lafferty and the colonel nodded at him.

Matt headed back through the waiting men. The sun beat down warmly on his back. The sky was a clear, flawless blue. Somewhere in the nearly silent town a child cried. A dog barked ceaselessly at the heels of the cavalrymen's horses across the square. There was the muted jangle of accouterments, the low murmur of talk among the civilian militia. But the voice of the governor was clearly audible. "Colonel, don't do this! Don't you realize what you're doing? You're heading an armed insurrection. Even if you win, the U.S. Army will hunt you down!"

Matt spoke softly as he passed among the men. "Fifteen or twenty of you come with me. Dismount and lead your horses back the way we came. We'll circle and get behind them on the other side."

He swung from his horse so that his departure would not be noticed. Others followed suit. Quietly, carefully, he led them away from the plaza, into the narrow streets beyond.

Once out of sight, he mounted and

spurred his horse into a gallop. With nearly a score of men behind him, he made a wide circle through the back streets a block from the public square.

Riding, his face grim and intent, Matt wondered if Lafferty could stall the governor long enough — long enough for him and his men to get set, on roofs, in windows, in any place that would command a clear view of the scene in the plaza.

On the far side of it, he yanked his horse to a halt, swung down, and tied the horse to a nearby rail. The others followed suit.

Running, rifle in hand, Matt led them along the narrow street toward the plaza. Half a block away they split, left and right, disappearing into an alleyway.

Matt and two others climbed to the roof of a lean-to and from there to the roof of a low, flat building. Crouching, they split, one to the right, one to the left. Matt ran forward between the two and crouched down behind the low adobe parapet facing the square. He was now looking down at the backs of the cavalry troop and militia. He rested his rifle on the parapet and waited silently.

Lafferty sat his horse in the center of the square, facing the governor, the lieutenant and Spahn. He roared, "I want my boy!

Give him to me and there will be no trouble!"

"He killed a man, Colonel," the governor replied. "He's been sentenced to die!"

"Give him to me or a hell of a lot of others are going to die before he does!"

The governor turned his head and looked helplessly at the lieutenant. Matt could see that the young man's face was white. But there was no retreat in it. The lieutenant shook his head.

The governor faced Lafferty again. "All right, Colonel. You win. I'll commute his sentence to life imprisonment. Is that what you want?"

Matt felt his breath run out in a long, slow sigh. It was a bigger concession than he had expected. It was more than Lafferty had expected too. He watched the colonel, his breathing stilled, and waited for Lafferty to nod his head.

Lafferty's eyes raised to scan the rooftops and windows behind the cavalry. He saw Matt and some of the others and suddenly he shook his head. "That ain't what I want and you damn well know it ain't. I want him free and I'll have him free."

The lieutenant spoke harshly. "Governor, we're wasting time. I'll scatter this rabble and that will be an end to it."

Matt jacked a cartridge into his rifle. The sound, coming clear and hard in the silence, made the lieutenant turn his head. The governor also turned to look.

When he spoke again, his voice held a pleading note. "For God's sake, Colonel Lafferty, be reasonable. You fought with this same cavalry during the war. Can you fight against it now?"

"Get back across the plaza, Governor. Unless you're prepared to pardon Link."

The governor stared at him for a moment. Then, his shoulders slumping, he turned and strode back across the plaza. His eyes, lifting, met Matt's briefly, hopelessly.

Lafferty rode back to his men, wheeled, and raised an arm. A ball of ice was growing within Matt's chest. He felt like a murderer. This was wrong and he knew it was wrong but he also knew that when the colonel dropped his arm he would begin firing. And with each shot a man would fall.

The arm dropped suddenly. Matt lowered his head and got one of the cavalrymen in his sights.

The plaza, the silent plaza, suddenly became a roaring battleground. Bluish powder smoke lifted into the still, clear air. Horses squealed with terror. Men tumbled from their saddles. Lafferty's men galloped in a ragged line toward the waiting cavalrymen.

Matt's point of aim was the center of a cavalryman's back. But he couldn't shoot. However he tried, he couldn't shoot.

He lifted his point of aim and shot the man's horse through the neck. He levered and fired again and another horse went down.

Caught between the fire of Matt's snipers and that of Lafferty's, the cavalry milled helplessly. Already half a dozen men were down. A dozen riderless horses galloped across the square and disappeared into one of the streets beyond.

Lafferty was going to win, thought Matt in amazement. He was actually going to win. In another minute or two it would be over. The cavalry would retreat and the militia would scatter and disappear. It would be over and the colonel would have won.

But suddenly something changed. From certain victory, Lafferty's men were unaccountably pulling back. They were wheeling their horses and galloping away.

The firing from the rooftops and windows on both sides of where Matt crouched slackened and stopped. He stared unbelievingly.

And then he understood. The colonel was no longer there. His riderless horse was one of a group of riderless horses galloping toward the far side of the square.

Matt felt as though he could not breathe. He stared across the plaza, frantically seeking Lafferty's body with his glance.

The two men on the roof with him got up and ran. He heard them jump to the lean-to roof but he did not turn his head. For he had found the colonel. . . .

Dropping his rifle, he got to his feet. He stared at the colonel an instant, his mind praying he would see the colonel move. He backed slowly away from the parapet.

Something slammed into his shoulder, spinning him halfway around. He staggered toward the rear of the roof, recovered and jumped to the lean-to roof below. He slid down it and dropped to the ground.

His shirt was already soaked with blood. His arm was numb. His head reeled and objects whirled crazily before his eyes.

He staggered into the street and along it to the plaza. In the confusion, he got through the milling crowd of militia and cavalrymen, got to the place he had seen Lafferty.

The colonel lay in the center of the plaza, upon almost the same spot the scaffold had stood so many years before. He lay completely still, in a crouched position. Beneath him, coloring the grass, soaking into the ground, was a pool of blood. Matt ran to his side and knelt.

Nausea crawled in his stomach as he stared unbelievingly. Lafferty had been literally cut to pieces. He was bleeding, or had been bleeding, from a dozen wounds. His clothing was soaked with blood.

Tears burned Matt's eyes and ran across his cheeks. He did not notice the sounds of battle stilled and died away.

There were voices now, audible in the stillness. Voices that were shocked, that did not believe. And there were other sounds, the groans of the wounded, the cries of those who wanted to surrender before they were shot down.

Matt got to his feet. Blood dripped off his fingertips. He saw the militiamen coming forward toward him, toward the other Two-Bar men. He heard Spahn's hoarse roar, "Hold it! Hold it right where you are! There'll be no killin' prisoners!"

He came to Matt, beside whom Les Saxon now stood. He looked down at Lafferty regretfully.

The governor approached, face white, hands and knees shaking violently. He too stared down at Lafferty.

The cavalrymen were rounding up the

prisoners. The governor stopped them when they came for Saxon and for Matt. "Let them be. Let them take him home."

Matt glanced at him gratefully. He wasn't sure how long he'd be able to stay on his feet. But he discovered that he could move his arm. At least the bone had not been smashed. He said numbly, "Les, see if you can find a buckboard for him."

Saxon mounted and rode away. The governor said, "I'm sorry, Matt. God, I'm sorry. He was a great man. But he died for nothing — for absolutely nothing."

Dr. Chavez appeared beside Matt and began cutting away his shirt, bandaging his wound. Spahn and the governor steadied him. Matt said weakly when Chavez had finished, "You'll want us, Spahn. We'll be at Two-Bar when you do."

Spahn nodded silently. Matt still had difficulty believing the colonel was dead. It seemed impossible that one so indomitable, who had endured so much and built so much, could be no more than a lump of dead flesh lying on the grass.

Les Saxon clattered along the street in a buckboard. He drove across the grassy plaza to where Lafferty lay, halted the rig and climbed down.

Unspeaking, the four moved to Lafferty's

body. Matt nearly fell when he stooped to help raise the colonel. He was forced to stand by helplessly while Spahn raised the colonel's head, while Saxon and the governor raised his feet. They laid him in the rig. When they had finished, the hands of all three were red with blood.

Matt climbed wearily into the rig. Saxon picked up the reins.

As they drove away, Matt glanced at the awed, silent crowd across the plaza. He looked at the dead and wounded lying scattered around like broken dolls. He stared at the Colonel's body lying behind him in the rig.

It was over now. The flame that had burned so brightly for so many years was ashes now. Colonel Lafferty was dead.

Slowly the buckboard rattled along, to the edge of San Juan and beyond, heading north toward Two-Bar ranch. The world reeled before Matt's eyes.

There would be consequences, he knew. For Saxon and for himself. There would be a trial and there would be penalties.

But he wasn't thinking of consequences. He was staring eagerly at a buggy coming toward them across the grassy plain.

When it reached them, Matt got down from the buckboard and watched it rattle away, heading north. Then he walked unsteadily toward Laura, who had gotten out and was standing on the ground. Her eyes were filled with tears, but they were tears of sympathy and joy. Gently, gently she put her arms around his waist.

For a long, long time they stared into each other's eyes. Tears ran across her cheeks and dropped, unheeded, to the ground. Her lower lip began to tremble uncontrollably.

Matt's own cheeks were wet. Suddenly his good arm went out and closed around her. He held her, this way, for a long, long time. As though he were never going to let her go.